"You may now kiss the bride."

Rab probably saw her panic because instead of kissing her, he started to speak. "I think we need to change this," he said, softly. "Mia, if you wish, and only if you wish… You may now kiss the groom."

There was a shocked hush in the tiny council chamber. Mia looked up into Rab's face and what she saw there… No pressure, his expression said.

And suddenly Mia found herself smiling.

Mia, if you wish, you may now kiss the groom.

She was suddenly thinking of this man's kindness and what he was doing to save her whole valley.

"Why not?" she whispered, raising herself on her tiptoes.

And she kissed him.

Dear Reader,

As someone who's been on the fringe of a medical life—"Reader, I married him"—I've heard many stories of patients enduring long convalescence after severe burns injury. I've thought after scarring and grafts, it must take sheer grit to face the world again—and that's what my heroine has in spades.

My Maira needed a true hero to match her zest for life, her loyalty and her courage—and I hope I've provided him in the form of Dr. Rab Finlay. Rab's a gorgeous hero, with a weakness for Mole and Toad, and all Kenneth Grahame's wonderful *Wind in the Willows* characters.

Dr. Finlay's Courageous Bride is a story of bravery, loyalty and romance with a capital *R*. I hope you love Maira's happy-ever-after as much as I do.

Marion

DR. FINLAY'S COURAGEOUS BRIDE

———

MARION LENNOX

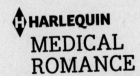

HARLEQUIN

MEDICAL ROMANCE

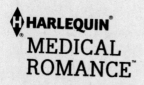

HARLEQUIN®
MEDICAL ROMANCE™

Recycling programs
for this product may
not exist in your area.

ISBN-13: 978-1-335-73739-7

Dr. Finlay's Courageous Bride

Copyright © 2022 by Marion Lennox

For questions and comments about the quality of this book, please contact us at CustomerService@Harlequin.com.

Harlequin Enterprises ULC
22 Adelaide St. West, 41st Floor
Toronto, Ontario M5H 4E3, Canada
www.Harlequin.com

Printed in U.S.A.

Marion Lennox has written over one hundred romance novels and is published in over one hundred countries and thirty languages. Her international awards include the prestigious RITA® award (twice!) and the *RT Book Reviews* Career Achievement Award for "a body of work which makes us laugh and teaches us about love." Marion adores her family, her kayak, her dog and lying on the beach with a book someone else has written. Heaven!

Books by Marion Lennox

Harlequin Medical Romance

The Baby They Longed For
Second Chance with Her Island Doc
Rescued by the Single Dad Doc
Pregnant Midwife on His Doorstep
Mistletoe Kiss with the Heart Doctor
Falling for His Island Nurse
Healing Her Brooding Island Hero
A Rescue Dog to Heal Them
A Family to Save the Doctor's Heart

Harlequin Romance

English Lord on Her Doorstep
Cinderella and the Billionaire

Visit the Author Profile page
at Harlequin.com for more titles.

This book is dedicated to all those who've found the courage to take control again, and to all those still struggling to find a way.

PROLOGUE

Sydney Central Hospital, twelve years ago

SHE DIDN'T KNOW who he was, but she didn't care.

She'd die without him.

Even in her head that sounded crazy, the sort of wild declaration she might have made as a twelve-year-old, swooning over pictures of rock stars in the magazines her mum brought home after cleaning Harvey's place. Harvey's girlfriends were always leaving magazines behind when they left, and she and her mum loved them. When Dad and Harvey were both away, her mum had sometimes seemed a kid herself, singing along with Maira's favourite songs and grinning at Maira's declarations of undying devotion to the gorgeous guys in the magazines.

That was so long ago now, though. The memory was like a stab of pain to the heart, adding to the pain from…everywhere.

But through the pain came his voice, soft, deep, steady.

"'Weasels—and stoats—and foxes and so on. They're all right in a way—I'm very good friends with them—pass the time of day when we meet, and all that—but they break out sometimes, there's no denying it, and then—well, you can't really trust them, and that's the fact.'"

She wasn't actually sure what a weasel was, or a stoat. She did know foxes—her dad used to shoot them—but that didn't matter. What mattered was that this man, this voice, was here in the small hours, when the hospital was deeply quiet, when apart from her hourly obs, the nurses let her be. She was supposed to be sleeping.

But how could she sleep? She drifted off when the meds kicked in, when the drugs gave her oblivion, but to sleep when she wanted seemed impossible.

But this deep, steady voice said that she might. His voice drifted around the quiet room, an oasis the nightmares couldn't touch.

Would the woman in the next bed feel the same? She must, she thought, for who wouldn't?

She'd figured it out by now—sort of. She was in a two-bed hospital ward. The lady in the next bed was called Hilda. The nurses had introduced them, even though neither of them could speak. 'Maira, this is Hilda who breeds champion Labradors. She was cooking dinner when she tripped over one of her puppies, knocking boiling water over herself as she fell. Her family tell us the puppy's fine, but Hilda's copped all the damage.'

Maira had heard the doctors talking to her—'The swelling will go down, Hilda. You'll be able to speak soon.'

Whereas for Maira…'The oil's burned your throat, Maira. It'll take time.'

She heard the subtle difference—there were no promises.

No future? She couldn't think of a future.

Hilda had visitors—her daughters even smuggled in the offending puppy. But Maira had no visitors, apart from the people from social services and the police.

She had nothing.

Only the sound of his voice.

Mr Toad. Ratty. Mole. Badger. She was starting to know them all.

There'd been other stories. He'd come in first a few nights ago, after a roster change. He'd been with the nurse, checking her chart, talking to her—*at* her?—about pain levels, describing what was happening. Then he'd come back.

'Hi, I'm Rab, here again, but not as a doctor. I'm on meal break, but who can eat at two in the morning? If there's drama outside I'll need to leave, but meanwhile I thought I'd do a bit of reading. How about it?'

Then, as he received no answer from either of them—how could he?—he'd settled on a chair between the beds.

'Okay, here we go. Sorry, guys, I know these are way beneath you, but I've pinched them from the kids' ward. Let's start with this first one—a mouse heading to sea in a stolen boat. It looks like fine literature to me, but stop me if you've read it. A twitch of a bandaged arm and I'll move right on to…ooh, the next is an elephant hatching an egg. Hmm, maybe we should start with this one?'

That had been a week ago. A couple of times he'd been interrupted—the door had opened—'Rab, you're needed in Room Five…'

'Excuse me, ladies, I'll be back.'

He'd kept his promise. He'd come back. She lay still now and let herself sink into the escape of his words.

'"*The Mole was bewitched, entranced, fascinated. By the side of the river he trotted as one trots, when very small, by the side of a man who holds one spellbound by exciting stories; and when tired at last, he sat on the bank, while the river still chattered on to him, a babbling procession of the best stories in the world, sent from the heart of the earth to be told at last to the insatiable sea.'''*

Did Hilda need this as much as she did? she wondered. Maybe so, for the older lady had been stirring and whimpering before he'd come in, but the stories seemed to work their magic on her as well.

Rab. He was Rab. Did he know how much he meant to her?

It wouldn't last. There'd be another roster change. He'd be needed elsewhere, of course he would. But the stories themselves... There'd been few books in her childhood home, but if her eyes started working again, maybe she could read.

Could she ever again?

There it was again, a jab of terror so fierce it cut through the pain. She heard him pause.

'Do you want me to stop?'

She managed to give her head a tiny shake, and there was a momentary pressure on her good arm.

'That's okay, Maira, just twitch this arm if you do. You're in control.'

That was a joke. She'd never been in control.

But the voice disagreed.

'From now on, Maira, the control's all yours,' the voice said, softly but surely. 'When you get through this, the world's your oyster. There are people who can help you, people who will. I promise. Now, where were we?'

He went back to the river with Mole, and while he read she let herself believe.

CHAPTER ONE

Cockatoo Valley Hospital

'I'M SORRY, BUT I believe the hospital will be sold.'

Silence. Twenty people were staring at him in horror, and Dr Rab Finlay was wishing himself anywhere but here.

Rab had asked for this meeting, but that didn't mean he wanted it. It would have been the easiest thing in the world to walk away, to tell himself this was nothing to do with him.

As indeed it wasn't. The consequences of his grandfather's will were dire for this little valley. Now he was facing almost the entire staff of Cockatoo Valley Hospital. They were looking sick with shock, but he couldn't change anything.

'I'm afraid there's nothing I can do,' he told them, trying to keep his voice steady. He'd been dreading this, and he wished now that he'd let the lawyers handle it. 'I haven't inherited my grandfather's land, so it'll pass to six of my relatives in England. I've been in touch with them. It seems they have little to do with each other, but as a group they want the land sold. The lease of the land the hospital sits on doesn't expire until next year, though,' he added. 'That may well give you time to apply for government assistance. The government may well buy it and keep the hospital running. I can help with the paperwork there, but that's all I can do. I'm sorry.'

'The government will never give us a grant big enough to match what the mining companies will pay. We'll lose our hospital.' That was Rhonda, the hospital secretary, sounding devastated.

Cockatoo Valley's elderly doctor, Ewan Baynes, had taken Rab for a brief tour of the hospital before this meeting, introducing him to each of the staff.

'I know you have no obligation to speak,' the shocked doctor had said heavily. Rab had explained the consequences of the will to him, and it had hit him hard. 'But everyone here knows how much we've been indebted to your family. Even though that's over, lives have been saved because of the Finlays—many lives. I believe everyone will want to meet you and pay their respects. Let's do that before we need to break the news.'

So Rab had endured a torturous half hour of meeting the hospital staff, being told how wonderful his forebears had been, how the hospital, the school, the church—the lifeblood of the valley—were all thanks to his family's generosity.

Then Ewan had organised a fast staff meeting so that Rab himself could break the news. At the last minute the elderly doctor had been called to an urgent house call, and Rab had thus faced the staff alone.

To tell them their hospital, their livelihood, even their community was being taken away from them.

'I can't see any way of avoiding it,' he said now. 'My grandfather's will is clear. The buildings on this side of the river are all on my grandfather's land—given to the community on a ninety-nine-year lease. I gather that even though my great-grandfather donated the buildings to the community, he still wanted control. That lease expires next year.'

'But we'll lose everything,' Rhonda said, sounding appalled. 'You know they want this valley for a coal mine. Most of our houses are over the bridge, on freehold land, but if they get this side of the river... They'll pay much more

for this land than we ever could. A coal mine...
Can't you stop that?'

'I can't.' There was nothing else to say. 'My
grandfather didn't leave the land to me.'

'Yeah, he did.' A voice piped up from the
back of the room, from a pimply-faced youth
who'd been introduced as a hospital orderly. The
kid stood up now and crossed his arms, belligerence personified. 'I knew this stuff,' he told
them. 'I saw it. Mum works at the local solici-
tor's, and she says wills aren't private. So she
had a look when the old guy died. The will
leaves it all to you.'

'Contents of the house only,' Rab told him.
'That's why I'm here, to take what I want and
then leave.'

'He left you the whole lot,' the youth threw
back at him. 'All you gotta do is to be married. Mum didn't know whether you were or
not. Are you?'

Help. He so didn't want to talk about his
grandfather's preposterous will—he'd hoped
he could simply say the place had not been left
to him. But the whole room was looking at him
now, waiting for an answer.

The stupid stipulation in the will meant the
destruction of this community, this valley. For
most of the people in this room—no, for all of
them—it meant not only the closure of the hos-

pital, the loss of jobs, it also meant the end of the community of Cockatoo Valley.

'I'm not married.' The three words were said with harsh finality.

'So get married.' The kid sounded angry. 'The will says you need to be married and settled before you're thirty-five. Mum looked you up on the internet—she says you're a doctor—she found you in some medical list. But Mum says you're only thirty-four. It didn't say if you were married or not, but she reckoned even if you weren't, if you stand to inherit all this then you'd get married pretty damn fast.'

'My birthday's in six weeks,' he told them. 'I'm sorry, people, but even for you I can't work that fast.'

There was another silence while they took the ramifications of that on board. The horror in the room was almost tangible.

'Surely you can find someone. If I wasn't already married with five kids I'd marry you myself.' It was Rhonda again, maybe trying to make light of an impossible situation.

'Thank you,' he said gravely. 'And indeed, if I had a fiancée, if there was the slightest chance of marriage, then I'd do it, but there's no way. I'm sorry but there's nothing more I can say.'

And then came the sound of a car, speeding along the road towards the hospital. They could hear a gunned engine, then tyres screeching as the car spun into the hospital driveway. Brakes hit hard, a voice yelling…

Four of the staff disappeared.

A hospital emergency. Rab knew the adrenalin of hearing such sounds—he'd worked in emergency departments himself, and he knew such an arrival meant total focus of the staff involved.

And for once he felt relieved. He needed the focus to be taken from him. It might sound harsh but there was nothing he could do about this mess. He didn't even know these people, this valley. His father might have been born here, but for Rab there was no connection.

The emergency outside seemed to have marked the end of the meeting. People wanted to be out of here, either to help with the incoming drama, or more likely to talk about the appalling repercussions of what he'd just said.

There was nothing left for him to do.

And then someone re-entered, pushing through the leaving staff. One of the nurses? He'd been introduced to this woman. Ewan had introduced them briefly—'This is our senior nurse, Mia, one of the most valuable members of our team.' He'd met so many but he remembered her—mostly because of the scars that marred one side of her face.

She was a striking woman, tall and slim, with long black hair braided down the back. She had a gorgeous tan—maybe a hint of Mediterranean background? Her wide grey eyes had smiled as she'd been introduced, and it was a lovely smile. But marring that smile were scars, sprawling down the left side of her face, down her neck and disappearing below the neckline of her uniform.

Burns, he'd thought as he'd met her. Old scarring. She must have been lucky to keep her sight, as the scarring started right against her left eye.

It must have been an appalling accident, he'd thought. A house fire? A car accident? The scarring was obvious, but she'd greeted him with a bright, light smile that took the attention from the disfigurement.

But there was no smile now. She was pushing through the departing staff, calling to him in a voice that was both urgent and authoritative. 'Dr Finlay?'

'Yes?'

'Ewan said you're a doctor,' she called. 'A people doctor?'

'I'm a surgeon.'

'Can you help then, please? The car that just arrived. It's a home birth gone wrong. We have a woman haemorrhaging postpartum, and she's in a bad way. As you know, Dr Baynes is on a house call on the far side of the valley, but we need a doctor. Please, if you will… We need you now.'

Mia had listened to Rab Finlay's announcement and felt sick.

From the time Angus Finlay had died, the community had tried to guess what would happen. The terms of the lease were well known. For years the community leaders, Ewan included, had tried to negotiate with the old man to change the terms of the lease, to somehow make the valley safe, but Angus hadn't been interested. As he'd aged he'd sunk into listless depression, and they couldn't break through it.

'I'll leave the place to my grandson,' he'd told them. 'I can't be bothered with all the legal stuff. He can do it.'

So there'd been uneasiness, but not total worry. Despite his depression, Angus had been in good health—even though he was in his eighties there'd been no sign that his death was imminent. 'I'm good for a few years yet, girl,' he'd told Mia the last time she'd seen him. She'd been assisting Ewan remove a skin cancer from his scalp.

'Well, how about wearing a hat and you might

live even longer,' Ewan had told him, and the old man had grunted disdain and headed out to the car park bare-headed.

And died of a massive infarct two weeks later.

But now…

Mia loved this valley, this community. It had taken her in, protected her, given her a life of safety and meaning. The thought of it being torn apart felt as if it was ripping the heart from her chest.

And it would be torn. There was another hospital at Colambool, an hour's drive down river. Colambool was a bigger town, but in this remote rural part of New South Wales even they struggled for government funding. The population of Cockatoo Valley would have to use it, though, she thought, as they'd have to use their school and church.

She thought of the cluster of houses on the other side of the bridge—most of them filled with retired farmers or alternative lifestylers. There was a general store over there, and a café, but without the hospital, church and school… would they stay?

Even if they did, they'd have to watch their beloved town being ripped up. This whole side of the river would be an enormous coal mine. To watch the destruction…

She'd been introduced to Rab Finlay and been impressed. In his mid-thirties, tall, dark, athletic, wearing branded chinos and an open-necked shirt that held the subtle hint of money and power, she'd been interested. When she'd heard what he'd had to say she'd been horrified. When the car had sped up to the Emergency entrance she'd almost been relieved to have to leave the meeting.

And then she'd walked out of the glass doors and any thoughts of the valley, of coal mines, of the loss of her community, were wiped from her mind.

The car pulling up at the entrance was an ancient Ford, pretty much a rust bucket. She recognised the car, and she knew the family spilling out. Tom Cray was in his forties, a helicopter pilot, sort of. He'd left the Air Force after some trauma he never talked of, bought a helicopter with his pay-out, and retired to the valley with his wife and kids. He took tourists on scenic flights, and businessmen to Sydney, but most of the time he devoted to his family. He and his wife, Isabelle, made weird things out of wire and set them up on the roadside, hoping to catch people's interest. Every now and then a passer-by would stop to take a look, but the pieces were big and weird, and the artists' propensity to leave bits of wire sticking out 'artistically' meant you were liable to take an eye out if you stumbled too close. They were also impossible to load into a car, so impromptu passers-by could hardly buy them on a whim.

But still Tom and Isabelle made them, while they scratched a living from their massive garden and occasional chopper flights. They also grew children—six of them, aged between two and twelve.

'I love having 'em, it's dead easy and why not?' Isabelle had told Mia last time she'd seen her. Isabelle had been heavily pregnant, but she hadn't come into Outpatients for an antenatal check—she'd brought eight-year-old Sunny in to have a gashed leg attended to.

Even then she'd come in reluctantly. The family didn't believe in doctors, and Isabelle certainly didn't believe in giving birth in hospital.

'They just pop out like peas out of a pod,' she'd told Mia happily. 'Dunno what all the fuss is about.'

There was fuss now. Tom was out of the car, hauling the back door open. A kid—the oldest... Marigold?—was climbing from the front seat, clutching a wrapped bundle—a baby?

Isabelle was lying on the back seat and the moment Tom opened the car door Mia saw blood.

A lot of blood.

'Baby came fast!' Tom was reaching in to his wife but yelling at Mia at the same time. 'No problems, a great little boy, and Isabelle was okay—and then she wasn't. Blood…she keeps bleeding. Mia, where's Doc?'

Doc Ewan. He was on the far side of the valley, Mia thought. Ray Markham's wife had rung for him to come. 'Ray's not able to get out of bed and he's struggling to breathe. His legs are so swollen. Can you get Doc to come?'

It'd be further heart trouble, they'd guessed, but there was no ambulance in the valley and Ray's wife was older than Ray's eighty. 'I'll contact the ambulance from Colambool and meet it there,' Ewan had decreed, and even though the elderly doctor had wanted to stay to hear Rab speak he'd had to go.

And now… One look at Isabelle told Mia there was no time to wait for Ewan. With this amount of blood, she needed a doctor, now!

Rab Finlay? Did she know him?

It was weird, but memories she'd long tried to put away had surfaced as she'd listened to Rab speak. His news had been shocking, but underlying his words, for her there'd been a sense of…familiarity? Peace? Calm?

It made no sense but, even if she was imagining things, Rab had been introduced as a doctor, and that was what she needed. Now.

'Get her out of the car and into Theatre,' she snapped at the staff behind her. 'IV line, plasma, move.'

She should send someone else to find Rab, but demanding his fast intervention was too important to leave to a junior. One look at Isabelle told her that finding a doctor right now was the only thing that stood between this woman and...

Don't think of it. Just go.

One minute he'd been a man imparting horrific news to an appalled community. The next he was thrust straight back into medical mode.

The woman who'd called him to come was Mia...someone? The nurse with the scarred face. She'd been the first to slip out when they'd heard the car screech to a halt outside.

But now she was standing in front of him. 'Please, if you will... We need you now.'

A woman haemorrhaging, postpartum... It could mean anything. A slight bleed, placental issues...

One look at this woman's face and he knew it wasn't. This was an experienced nurse, and her face said...fear.

No other doctor? Hell.

'Will you come?'

There was no choice. He was already ripping off his jacket.

'I'm with you,' he said and headed for the door.

CHAPTER TWO

THE FIRST SIGHT of Isabelle had left Mia almost sick with dread. This was no minor bleed—nothing that stitching and an IV drip could handle. This was something major—something horrific.

A ruptured uterus? It was an explanation she didn't want to think about, but she must. The diagnosis was only a dread, but it was suddenly front and foremost.

Isabelle was in her early forties—'Tom and I met late, we're making up for lost time,' she'd told Mia once when Mia had talked to her about her kids. This was her seventh birth. If there'd been wear to the uterus, with the strain of the birth, a tiny tear could suddenly turn catastrophic.

Mia had checked the baby—very briefly. He was hugged tight in twelve-year-old Marigold's arms. The baby looked okay. 'Take Marigold into the kids' ward and check the baby,' she'd told Issy, the most junior nurse. Issy was young but smart. She could be trusted to yell if there were any problems, so that meant all their attention could be on Isabelle.

All Rab's attention...

He was here now, supervising as the trolley was being wheeled into Theatre. Steadily but calmly questioning Tom. 'Focus, mate,' he said. He was inserting an IV line as the trolley moved. 'Age? How many previous births? How long's she been bleeding? Are there any medical conditions that could cause bleeding? Do you know her blood group?'

'Forty-three,' Tom managed. 'No...no health conditions. She's been bleeding for half an hour—I thought it was just normal—but all of a sudden it got worse. And I don't know her blood group.'

'Rhonda will make a call to Colambool,' Mia said quietly, matter-of-factly. 'They have a blood bank. They can send a fast car with O neg blood. It'll take a while though.'

He nodded. 'Plasma expander will do for now, then. That's great, Tom.'

Tom was walking behind the trolley, his hand holding Isabelle's, as if he let go she might well drown. He looked panicked, but Rab's steady questioning seemed to have given him direction.

'She's been okay,' he told him. Seventh kid,

home birth like always and bub came out just like they all do. All normal but then the blood... Couldn't think... Just picked her up and carried her to the car...'

'You've done well, mate,' Rab told him. He was looking down at Isabelle. Her face was deathly white, her eyes wide with fear. 'Isabelle, we have you safe now,' he told her. 'But you're bleeding a bit too much to be normal. I'm guessing it's probably a tear, a rip that the baby's made coming out.' His voice gentled a little. 'Isabelle, is it okay if we put you to sleep and fix it?'

'Just do it,' Tom broke in, but Rab took Isabelle's spare hand and held.

'You're in control, Isabelle,' he told her. 'What we do is up to you. But I think your uterus might be damaged. If I operate...we may need to remove the whole thing. That's a hysterectomy. If we need to do that to stop the bleeding, is that okay?'

'I...yeah.' It was a faint whisper. 'Seven kids. Don't need the bloody thing any more.'

'Bloody's right,' Rab said and smiled. 'Great, Isabelle, we'll get this sorted. 'Tom, you need to sign some forms. Can you let one of these people take you to the office? Isabelle, we're putting you to sleep now so we can fix the bleeding and then get you back together with your new baby. Right?'

'R...right,' Isabelle whispered as someone swung open the doors to Theatre and she was wheeled through.

But for a moment Mia stood stunned, motionless.

'You're in control, Isabelle.'

After all these years, the words were still with her, a whisper of the past. A turning point.

'You're in control.'

The faint echoes of recognition she'd already felt coalesced into certainty. She knew this man.

But there was no time for thinking this through. She gave a faint gasp and then gave herself a mental shake. Her past didn't matter now. Rab would need all the help he could get if he was to save Isabelle's life.

Maybe he'd saved her life, but it shouldn't stop her from helping him save another.

The last thing he'd intended when he'd walked into this hospital this morning was to turn back into a surgeon, but he clearly had no choice.

He wasn't an obstetrician for a good reason— obstetrics had always seemed to him to be a profession of ninety-nine percent boredom, one percent panic.

He had obstetric colleagues and they enjoyed the process, the emotion, the waiting, as expectant women were transformed into mothers, usually caring, loving, totally committed from the start. For Rab the emotion always left him uncomfortable.

His own mother had been...well, absent. She'd left him with his father when he was a baby, and had rebuffed any attempt to make contact. Rab's father had been a loner who had little time for anyone, and he'd merely shrugged when Rab had asked about her. 'She was a mistake, boy. I don't need her, and neither do you.'

Rab had thus been raised by a succession of nannies. He couldn't miss what he'd never had, but still, the sight of a new mum holding her baby as if it were the most precious thing in the world had always left him with a sense of loss. General surgery had seemed far less fraught, a place where he could help but emotions could usually take a back seat.

Despite that, his training had included obstetric surgery. He guessed what he was facing now, and speed had to be of the essence.

He needed a surgical team. Assistants. An anaesthetist...

Ewan was clearly nowhere nearby. He was on his own.

'I can give the anaesthetic.' Mia was speaking calmly across Isabelle's trolley, as if this was almost routine. 'Ewan's the sole doctor here, and we've had emergencies before. He's trained me. I need orders but if you tell me what to do, I'll do it. Isabelle, you're okay. We have you safe.'

Her words seemed to steady Isabelle. They also steadied him.

'Any history?' She'd know the drill.

'No pre-existing that I know of. Seventh home birth. No antenatal care. But Isabelle's fit and strong, aren't you, Isabelle?'

'I can... I need to live.' The woman's voice was thready.

'Of course you do,' Mia said steadily. 'And we're here to make it a certainty.'

'But this isn't Doc Ewan...' There was still panic.

'No, but this is Dr Rab Finlay, and making sure people live is his specialty. I've known him for ever, and I know you're in safe hands. Promise. We're popping an anaesthetic in now, so lie back and go to sleep. When you wake up, the bleeding will have stopped and you'll have your gorgeous baby to hold and to love. Trust us, Isabelle.'

And Isabelle gripped her hand as if she were drowning and managed to whisper, 'Thank God you're both here. Oh, thank God...'

* * *

What followed was surgery that required all the skill he possessed—and more. But his initial sense of panic as he'd thought of the enormity of operating without any backup had been almost instantly dispelled as Mia reassured him, and as the surgery commenced the panic didn't reappear.

A ruptured uterus was the worst kind of obstetric nightmare. With the amount of blood loss, it was amazing that she'd made it to hospital. That she was still alive, that her vital signs were holding…

Her continued survival was down to him, but it was also down to the team around him.

As far as he could see he had two trained nurses, Mia and a younger one, but there were people in the background. The woman who'd been on the desk when he'd arrived—Rhonda—was passing equipment through the door. An elderly man dressed in hospital blues was clearing as they worked, silently taking used bags, equipment, following Mia's soft orders. The junior nurse—Marie?—was handing him whatever he needed, usually instinctively, though sometimes Mia prompted her—always before he had time to throw the order himself.

And Mia herself seemed almost as good as a trained anaesthetist, he thought. He'd outline dosages, give instructions, but thirty seconds into his orders he'd realise that she had a grip on the situation. That she knew not only dosages but what was at stake—that the woman they were working on was in danger of cardiac arrest, that the blood loss had to be arrested fast, that as well as administering anaesthetic and supporting ventilation she had to watch monitors, warn him of any faltering…

The surgery was pushing him to the extent of his skills. He was a general surgeon, not a gynaecologist, and the moment he'd made the first incision he'd realised the tear to the uterus was extending with pressure from the blood loss itself. It must have started small, he thought, or she'd never have made it this far.

But she had plasma on board now, and that and the saline would be holding her blood pressure steady. The O negative blood—the universal group used when fast cross-matching wasn't possible—would arrive soon. They might just manage it.

Thank God she'd made it to hospital, he thought. Thank God for this team.

He was about to close this hospital down.

There was no time to think about that now, but it stayed in his mind, a shadow as he worked. And as he accepted that Isabelle had every chance of surviving, somehow the shadow grew darker.

There was nothing he could do about it. If he could turn back time, speak to his grandfather before he'd died...

Well, maybe that wouldn't have worked either, he decided as he finally managed to get things under control. Rab had met his grandfather for the first time at his father's funeral. The old man had barked questions at him, had obviously disliked his answers and that had been the extent of their relationship.

The will, with its crazy stipulation, had come as a bolt from the blue, but it shouldn't have mattered too much to him. He hadn't expected an inheritance. He was well off himself, he didn't need the money that such an inheritance would bring. The stipulation that he must be married was impossible to fulfil anyway. He'd come to the valley to let them know in person, because it had seemed the honourable thing to do, but now...

Now he had misgivings. Doubts. Consequences he'd never thought of.

He looked down at the woman he'd just operated on. Without a hospital here...

She'd make it, he thought. He was closing now. The uterus was cleared, the final stitches were being inserted, the thing was done.

He gave Mia orders for reversal of anaesthesia and felt his breathing return to normal.

'She should never have had a home birth,' he said, almost to himself. 'With only this hospital in reach… No backup…'

'She would have had a home birth even if this hospital didn't exist,' Mia told him. 'But she'd have died.' She was still watching Isabelle's breathing. She'd removed the endotracheal tube, but it seemed she wasn't taking chances. 'And it's not just incidents like Isabelle being stubborn where we're needed. We service a huge rural area, and accidents happen. Colambool's an hour's drive to the north, but to the south there's nothing. So if there's an accident half an hour south of here, then it's half an hour before we can reach them or they can get to us, and then at least another hour for transfer.' She closed her eyes for a brief moment but then opened them and shook her head, as if she were shaking off a bad dream. 'Still, as you explained, there's nothing you can do.'

'If I'd known I might even have married,' he said, almost to himself, but she shook her head.

'This isn't your call. And maybe… Well, Doc Baynes is over seventy now. He's an awesome doctor but he's slowing and no one wants to take his place. Maybe the hospital would have closed anyway.'

'But not the school and the church as well.'

'As you say.' She sighed. 'I... Can I leave you now? Tom'll be out of his mind with worry. It'd be best if you talk to him—I hope you do—but I wouldn't want both of us to leave yet and... and you have the skills if...'

'There's no *if.* Tell him there's every chance she'll be okay,' he said, a bit too roughly. He was watching the monitors, seeing the steadying of the heartbeat, the blessed rising of blood pressure as plasma intake finally compensated. Yes!

'I'll do that,' she told him. 'And Rab...thank you.'

'You can hardly thank me,' he said roughly. 'Seeing I'm destroying your hospital.'

'It's not your fault,' she told him. 'No one can force anyone else to marry. Ever.'

And she gave a brief decisive nod and headed out to give Tom the good news.

Ewan returned to the hospital an hour later. The elderly doctor was emotional already, and even more so when he heard what had happened in his absence.

'I can't thank you enough,' he told Rab. 'Tom and Isabelle—their lifestyle wouldn't suit most of us but they're great people, great parents. It would have ripped the hearts out of all of us if Isabelle had died.'

'As it will if this hospital closes.' Rab was feeling ill. 'I'm so sorry.'

'Nothing you can do about it, son,' Ewan said roughly and clapped him on the shoulder. 'But thanks for being here today. Not just for Isabelle—thanks for having the courage to come and tell us in person.' And then he hesitated. 'Isabelle… I'm not sure… Maybe I should transfer her to Sydney?'

Rab heard the uncertainty, an elderly general practitioner alone with a patient who'd been near to death. There might well be complications. Ewan suddenly sounded weary beyond his years.

And Rab heard himself say, 'I'll be here for a while. My grandfather left the contents of the house to me, so I'll stay and sort it. There are family papers, things I need to organise, and I'm happy to help out with Isabelle if I can. I think it's safe enough not to transfer. If there are problems I'm a phone call away.'

'For how long?'

'Maybe a week. Isabelle will be fine by the time I leave.'

'And then?' And all of them knew what Ewan's question meant.

But there was only one answer. 'I'm sorry,' Rab said gently. 'I can do no more.'

And that was that. He walked out to the car park feeling a bleakness that was bone deep.

And from the window at the rear of the nurses' station Mia watched him go. And thought…

Control.

Why was that word suddenly front and centre?

She was thinking, weirdly, of her past. Of her childhood in a tiny rural community, almost completely cut off from the world outside. Of her father, who was a coward and a bully. Of her mother, a downtrodden wisp of a woman who never dared raise her voice, who never disagreed with her husband over anything. Of her father's friends, and of the overarching community hierarchy that assumed she, as a woman, had no control over anything.

She was thinking of herself at seventeen, inspired by books from spasmodic visits of a local library van, but more, she was inspired by hope, by the need to fledge her wings, by the desire to escape. *'I want to go to university.'*

She was thinking of her father's derision, and then the slaps. 'You'll marry, and you'll marry Harvey. Be grateful he wants you. Think of the money he makes and that great house he lives in. You're a lucky girl—all you have to do is keep him happy.'

She recalled her disbelief, her determination to leave. But then her mother: 'If you leave, I'll be alone. Maira, I can't live if you leave as well.'

And eventually, in the face of her father's bullying, her mother's sobs, she'd caved in. She'd married. But of course Harvey wasn't a 'good catch'. He'd wanted her as a possession, there to pleasure him.

She was thinking of the threats, the violence, her inability to please, no matter how she tried. Of her mother coming one day and finding her beaten, sobbing, distraught. Her mother trying to take her away.

Harvey's threat: 'She's mine and I keep my own, no matter what it takes. Leave or you'll get what she's already had.'

And then, at nineteen, that last awful night. He'd been drunk. She'd made fish and chips for their dinner but the chips were soggy. The fat hadn't been hot enough.

It hadn't been hot enough for the chips, but it was hot enough for...

Don't go there, she told herself, but she already was. Her hand raised instinctively to the scars etched across her cheek.

Control.

This valley had given it back to her, she thought. Ewan's daughter, Robyn, had been a social worker at the hospital and she'd helped her, organising her safe refuge after she'd left hospital, then—maybe against professional principles—she'd brought her to Cockatoo Valley to recover.

Doc Ewan and his wife had guided her back to health with their gentle care. She'd taken a new name—Maira had become Mia. The whole valley had seemed to surround her, shielding her from the trauma of the trial, Harvey's imprisonment, even lessening the shock of her mother's death.

The community had also scraped enough for a scholarship for her to attend university, to train as a nurse, but the valley had always been her refuge whenever there was a break in her studies. Always there'd been the assurance that Cockatoo Valley was her home.

It'd be lost.

Control.

Rab had reached his car now, but he didn't climb in. He stood and looked back at the hospital building, then seemed to look further, his gaze sweeping over the backdrop of gentle hills, the lush pastures that'd soon be swallowed by a giant coal mine.

Control.

Could she?

This was her valley. Her home. It was her choice, and she knew it.

She looked out at Rab for a long moment and memories came flooding back. The sound of his voice in the night. His words, a mantra that had echoed ever since.

From now on, Maira, the control's all yours.

Enough. She left the room and started to run.

CHAPTER THREE

HE WAS STANDING by the car when he saw her running towards him. Isabelle? he thought, his heart sinking. What had happened? Cardiac arrest? It wasn't unthinkable after such huge blood loss. He started towards her but she stopped, maybe three metres away. Almost skidding to a halt. Seeming breathless.

She was still dressed in her theatre scrubs, blue pants and smock and the plastic clogs that were easy to clean. Her face was devoid of make-up. Her long plait of silky black hair had been under a cap in Theatre. It hung free now and he suddenly thought he'd missed it. Her clear grey eyes were wide and direct. Apart from the faded scars on the left side of her face and neck, her skin was flawless and her...

Oh, for heaven's sake, what was he thinking? Get a grip.

'What is it?' he asked a bit too brusquely. 'Isabelle?'

'No, she's fine. At least…okay. Doc's with her. I just wanted…to talk to you.' She still sounded out of breath, and there was a long pause, as if she were fighting to recover.

The hospital entrance was less than fifty metres away. Why did she sound as if she'd just run a race?

'Sorry,' she said at last. 'But I don't know how to say this.'

'Say what?' Now his concern for Isabelle was allayed he was intrigued. He leaned back against the car and waited for her to collect herself.

Which she did. She almost visibly braced, squared her shoulders and asked, 'How much do you want to save the valley?'

'I can't.'

'No, if you could…how much do you value it?'

What was she getting at?

'I've never thought about it,' he conceded. 'At least, not until I heard the contents of my grandfather's will. I hardly knew him, and I had no expectation of an inheritance. This is the first time I've seen it.'

'It's special.'

'I imagine most people think their home's special.'

What did she want? To plead with him to somehow save it? It wasn't possible.

'It must be possible to save it,' she said, disagreeing with his unvoiced thought. 'There *must* be some way. Look at it. Can you imagine all this as a coal mine?'

He couldn't. That was what he'd been thinking as he'd stood by the car, taking a moment before he left to gaze around him.

Gardens had been developed right down to the river's edge, the river bank denoting the boundary of the hospital grounds. Towering eucalypts grew along the river bank, with sweeping lawns and native flora forming a magnificent garden leading right up to the hospital veranda.

Birds were everywhere. Seats were scattered, some in sun, some in shade. His great-grandfather had been more than generous in allocating hospital land, he thought, and he remembered the lease he'd looked at briefly. It seemed that maintenance had been included in the contract—these gardens must have been funded until now by…his family.

The thought that this place was his family's legacy was disturbing. He had no real concept of the generations of Finlays who'd settled here, who'd made their fortune from this land, who'd called this place home.

He allowed himself now to gaze further, at

the cluster of homes and businesses on the far side of the river. They overlooked this place, the magnificent hospital grounds, the river itself and then further, to the gentle hills beyond, the lush grazing land. This was all destined to be ripped up to provide coal.

The thought was almost obscene—and this woman was looking at him as if she expected him to do something about it.

'I am sorry,' he said again, gently, regretfully. 'But there's nothing I can do.'

'You could marry.'

'In six weeks?' He gave a mirthless laugh. 'What do you expect me to do? Advertise?'

'There must be someone. A girlfriend...'

'No,' he said dryly, thinking of Skye, the dippy, funny nurse he'd been spending a bit of time with lately. Their attraction was superficial, though. Skye was about to head to London on the start of an adventure, working her way around the world. They were little more than friends—light-hearted lovers? And even if he asked and she agreed, there was another stipulation to the will: *married and happily settled.*

'You'd need to be together for at least a year,' his grandfather's lawyer had told him, not entirely unsympathetic. 'That would mean living together—at least until the lease expires and everything's settled.'

Skye, settled?

Him, settled?

The idea was laughable.

'So...how much do you want it?' the woman in front of him demanded. And then she corrected herself. 'Sorry, that sounds pushy but... how much do you think you could care?'

'I can't...'

He'd started to say he didn't care at all, but something stopped him. The sun was on his face and the birds were all around him. The hospital, built of mellowed local sandstone, with long verandas, French windows looking out over the river, gracious sun lounges—this was the most perfect place for a hospital.

And the setting. The little school he could see in the distance. The church. The magnificent grazing land.

He thought of it being destroyed, ripped up to become a massive, open cut coal mine. How much did he want to save it?

The woman before him squared her shoulders even more and asked, 'Enough to marry me?'

What followed was a silence that stretched out and out, continuing as if each was afraid to break it.

He was looking at her as if she had two heads.

Well, she was used to being stared at, she conceded. Her scars had faded over time, becoming little more than a series of whitish tracks and a flattening where grafted skin had reduced the capacity of her face to produce life lines. But the memory of those early years was still with her, the failure of people to hide their shock. She occasionally still got it, from people who saw her first from the unmarred side and then were hit by the scarring as she turned.

But Rab's gaze wasn't on the scars. He was searching her eyes. Like a doctor looking for signs of psychosis.

'It's just a thought,' she said at last, a bit too brusquely. 'A possibility. I mean…if you really do want to save the valley… I'm not married and I could agree to whatever conditions you had. Or… I guess…depending on the conditions.' She was talking too fast, and she was trying to sound offhand, as if it was a small thing she was offering. Asking?

'I think it could work, as long as I kept control,' she added quickly. 'As…as long as we both kept control, set boundaries, knew what we were letting ourselves in for.' Because that was the biggie, the stipulation that had hit her the minute the idea had come into her head. This had to be on her terms. She'd had enough of other people's terms to last her a lifetime.

He was staring at her with a mixture of bemusement and shock. 'But…why?' He sounded confounded.

'Because I care about this valley.'

'Is that all? What's in it for you?'

And that brought a flash of anger. And another memory. Of her father standing over her, yelling.

'You'll be living in that great house. All you have to do is shut up and submit and you'll get everything you want.'

Right.

She closed her eyes, and suddenly Rab's hand was on her arm. And when she opened her eyes again she saw…concern?

'Mia, what is it?' His voice was gentle. 'I'm seeing grief here. What do you stand to lose if this valley's sold?'

The nightmare receded. This was nothing to do with Harvey, with her past. It was…the opposite.

'Everything,' she managed, and fought to find the words to explain. His hand stayed on her arm and she didn't pull away. 'I… Maybe that's not true. If this valley disappears, I'm a trained nurse. I have no roots. I could move away. Start a new life somewhere. But these people…they're my people.'

'Your family?'

'I don't have family.' She said it harshly. 'I

have the community that embraced me after my…after I was burned. They cared for me, made my life mean something again, and I'll do whatever it takes to protect them. As long as I can stay…me.'

'As long as you can keep control?' He must have heard the way she'd said the word, as if it was everything.

'Yes.'

'Mia, how could you possibly trust me enough to marry me?'

And there it was, said out loud, the question that was so huge it took her breath away.

And there was only one answer.

'Because once upon a time you read me *The Wind in the Willows*.'

'*The Wind in the Willows*?'

She fought for an explanation, knowing she had to explain because this memory, this slight thing that had seemed so huge for her, was the final reason she'd found enough courage to… propose?

'In the burns unit of Sydney Central, almost ten years ago,' she stammered. 'Late at night. Me and Hilda. A two-bed ward and neither of us could see. I was badly burned and so was Hilda, and the nights were awful. But you came in, night after night—sometimes for a little, sometimes for longer. You were there until I was moved to rehab. It probably meant little to you, but for Hilda and me it was everything. What you did for us—your voice. Rab, I was so close to...to not wanting to go on, but you reminded me there was kindness in the world. You were the first, and then the people of this valley took over. It's a debt, you see, and you're a part of it. So if you could use me...under my terms...'

There was a call from the door of the hospital. She turned and a nurse was beckoning. 'Mia!'

'Sorry, I need to go,' she told him. 'And...and I'm sorry. What I've just said, it's probably ridiculous. You'll probably reject it out of hand, but that's okay. Or it's not okay but it's your right. I just...had to try.'

She pulled a slip of paper from her pocket and handed it over. 'Here's my phone number in case, but otherwise forget I said it. Thank you for *The Wind in the Willows*, if nothing else.'

And she turned and walked quickly back into the hospital without looking back.

He headed out to the homestead, Wiradjuri—it was the indigenous word for kookaburra. That was where he'd been heading. He'd called into the hospital almost as a courtesy, but there was nothing more he could do.

Except think of what Mia had said.

It was a crazy proposition, so crazy he could

do nothing but put it out of his mind while he sorted the next thing.

The homestead was set about a kilometre away, around the river bend from the township. Like the hospital, it was built of the local sandstone. Like the hospital, it was gorgeous.

His great-grandparents must have had magnificent taste, he thought, as he drove along the sweeping curve that led to the house. The gardens here were even more fabulous than the hospital's. They were low maintenance, mostly native, but a wonderful blend of nature versus nurture.

An elderly woman, wiry, grey hair caught in a loose bun, dressed in overalls and wellingtons, was on her hands and knees, digging clumps of what looked like weeds from along the garden path. As Rab's car pulled up she rose and he saw bulbs at the ends of the dried stalks.

'Daffodils,' she said briefly. 'Millions of 'em. I'm thinning 'em, cleaning up spares for the school fair.' And then she paused, her brows snapping together. 'Oh, wait. You'll be the new owner, then. Mr Finlay?'

'Rab.'

'Wow, finally.' She grimaced. 'I'm Nora, gardener here for ever, or until the place is sold. Your grandpa told me about you. Married then?'

So she knew the stipulation of the will and was cutting right to the chase.

'No.'

She swore, a loud expletive that seemed to shake the peace of the valley. Then her eyes narrowed. 'You intending to do something about it?'

'There's nothing I can do. My birthday's in six weeks.'

She swore again. 'I told him,' she muttered. 'Your grandpa.' She reached out a filthy hand and shook his, disregarding the dirt. 'Angus mostly kept to himself, but he told me years ago, after your dad died, when he realised you were still single. "He'll be happily married or he won't inherit," he told me, and I kept telling him to check whether you were or not, because I'm sure he decided that in anger. Angus didn't even know those relations he had in England, and he didn't reach out to contact you. But of course he thought there was all the time in the world.'

Her face clouded a little. 'He was just…upset, you know, thinking you were turning out like your dad. So he put a gun to your head but didn't even let you know. What an idiot.' She hesitated. 'So what happens now?'

'The cousins will inherit and the place will be sold.'

The colour drained from her face. 'The whole valley…'

'Just this side of the river.'

'Makes no difference. The valley'll be stuffed.' She swallowed a few times and then turned and looked out over the river. 'Strewth, isn't there anything you can do? You can't… I dunno… marry fast?'

'Nora…'

'I know, it's none of my business,' she told him, her voice trembling. 'And, to be fair, I guess it's none of yours. Maybe even if you married you'd sell anyway. It's too late for your grandpa to order you into anything. So what… what are you here for?'

'I need to check the contents.'

'Fine,' she said, sniffing. 'Do you have a key?'

'The lawyer gave me one.'

'I'll let you get on with it then,' she said, and she could no longer disguise her tears. She compressed her lips and stared out past the garden, towards a massive clump of briars sprawled over the bank just beyond the river bend. When she spoke again he could see she was struggling to sound matter-of-fact.

'Okay. Moving on. I might poison those blackberries before someone else takes over. Your grandpa loved the berries, and the local kids pick them too. But they're a noxious weed and I struggle to control them. Cutting them back's a filthy job, and if the coal mine ignores them they'll take over the whole damned valley.' She gulped. 'Not that... I guess...maybe it doesn't even matter.' She stared down at her heap of lifted bulbs. 'And I might as well take all of these daffodils. They'd never survive a coal mine.'

And she turned her back, stooped and started digging again. Conversation over.

He felt ill, but what could he say? There was nothing.

The front door key was huge, a great iron key tied with string to a worn wooden...frog? It looked as old as the house itself, but surely his great-grandparents didn't cart around carved frogs.

He knew little about his great-grandparents—or his grandparents either, for that matter. All he knew of his family was that his father, Douglas, had been a twin. His twin, Donald, had drowned in the river when the boys were twelve, and Douglas had been blamed. That blame seemed to have been bone deep. The young Douglas had been packed off to boarding school, to university, to life, with parental money but little else. He'd graduated with honours, become a wealthy financier, moved from woman to woman, been landed with an unwanted son from one of those liaisons—that'd be Rab—but had never seen the need to come home. Neither had he seen the need to introduce his son to his parents.

So Rab walked into the homestead now expecting to feel that this place was nothing to do with him. But as he walked through the faded grandeur of the entrance hall and into the sitting room the first thing that caught his eye was a portrait hanging over the marble fireplace.

Two small boys, obviously twins, arms linked, cheeky grins. Two boys seemingly ripe for adventure.

Douglas and Donald? His father and his uncle?

He stood in the doorway and felt his gut lurch. His grandparents must have spent what was left of their lives looking at this every day. One son lost through tragedy, the other through choice.

His father had hardly talked of it, but once, late at night after an evening's heavy drinking, he'd told Rab about his twin.

'He drowned and I couldn't help him,' he'd said. 'And it almost destroyed me, so let it be a lesson to you. You stand on your own two feet, boy. You don't need anyone.'

He drowned and I couldn't help him.

The phrase drifted through Rab's mind now

as he looked at the photograph, and for some reason it seemed to be echoing. Growing louder?

His grandmother had died here twenty years ago, and his grandfather had lived on alone. Rab went from room to room, seeing faded grandeur. It was as if the house had been almost closed up when the boys were gone, maintained but not changed. A couple had lived here, presumably loved, had twins, lost one then rejected the other. And then...nothing?

The library downstairs was the only room that looked lived in, with papers on the fireside table, a coat draped over an overstuffed settee. The kitchen looked cold and unwelcoming. An Aga was set into the fireplace, but a two-ring electric burner, stained with wear, said the Aga had seldom been used.

The place was musty, cold, almost repelling. It was as if the occupant of this house had died fifty years ago, instead of two weeks back.

The sadness... The grief...

He drowned and I couldn't help him.

He headed up the wide staircase to the bedrooms beyond. One room was bright, cheerful, or it would have been if not for the faded wear that came from age. Huge windows looked out over the valley. Boxes of toys were still scattered, the sort of things twelve-year-olds would love.

Two beds were carefully made.

For some reason anger was swelling. What a waste. He got it all—his father's remoteness, his grandfather's appalling will, the stubbornness that had wrecked four lives after the tragedy of one.

Below the window Nora was shoving her spade into the dirt with a fierceness that was surely unnecessary. Her shoulders were shaking. He could almost bet that she was still crying.

This place. This valley. It would go. A whole community destroyed by the bitterness of the past.

He drowned and I couldn't help him.

Enough. He pulled up the window and leaned out. 'Nora?'

She looked up, startled. 'I… Yes?'

'Don't take all of those bulbs away. Not yet.'

There was a moment of stillness. 'You mean…?'

'I have no idea what I mean,' he told her. 'Just leave them be.'

And then he tugged the slip of paper from his pocket and looked at the number.

Mia. A woman he didn't know.

She answered on the first ring, almost as if she'd been waiting.

'Could you come out to the homestead? I… We need to talk.'

There was no hesitation. 'Yes.' Then there was a moment's pause. 'I bet there's no food in the house. You want me to bring fish and chips?'

The note of practicality grounded him. Sort of. One part of him was on shifting sands, the rest knew exactly what he was doing.

'That'd be great,' he told her.

'See you soon then,' she said, and she almost sounded cheerful. As if what was happening was good?

What *was* happening?

He stood at the window of his father's childhood bedroom. He stared over the valley and he had no idea.

CHAPTER FOUR

DRIVING OUT TO the Finlay homestead was probably the hardest thing Mia had ever had to do.

Was she out of her mind? After all these years, to put her head in the noose again…

But this time it'd be on her terms, she told herself, and no, it wasn't putting her head in a noose. It'd be Rab who'd be losing control.

Or both of them taking it?

The road wound along the river. It was early autumn, a gorgeous still night. Cattle—mostly red and white Herefords—were grazing lazily in the paddocks. River redgums shadowed the river, welcome swallows were flitting over the water and herons were wading along the edges.

The valley's beauty was enough to take her breath away. It was enough to risk…everything?

If it hadn't been Rab she could never have considered it, she conceded. This valley had to be saved, but if it hadn't been Rab she'd never have found the courage.

But that thought brought another qualm, and a big one. She was acting as if she knew the guy, and in truth the only knowledge she had of him was a voice in the darkness, dispelling the appalling nightmares.

And now she wanted him to dispel still more. The nightmare of this valley's destruction.

'Am I being a total fool?' She said the words aloud and the dog on the passenger seat beside her turned his head and looked at her as if puzzled. Well, Boris was almost permanently in a state of puzzlement. He was a great lump of a dog, a cross between a boxer and a mastiff. Maybe with a bit of bloodhound in there as well? He had a smooth brown coat, long, long legs, floppy ears, and eyes that looked out on the world as if it was the most exciting thing he'd ever seen—even if he'd seen the same thing two minutes earlier.

Robyn had given him to her as a puppy, when she'd moved back here and decided to rent a little house just for her—the first time she'd lived alone for... Well, since Harvey. Harvey was safely in jail, but protection had still been in her mind. Well, that idea had been a joke. Boris would lick any attacker to death, she thought, but he was frankly adorable and he made her happy.

Harvey was due for release soon. Maybe she needed to get something else for protection.

Another name? She'd changed it once. To do it again could be a double protection.

She could change it via marriage this time, instead of by deed poll.

No. She was not doing this for her own sake, she told herself, but a little voice whispered… it couldn't hurt.

She pulled into the driveway. Rab was sitting on one of the old cane chairs on the veranda and the sight of him had all her qualms rushing back in force.

What was she doing?

But he was rising, walking down the steps to meet her, and it was too late to pull back. He was smiling a greeting. He was…gorgeous. She'd thought he was good-looking when Ewan had introduced him back at the hospital, but now…

Hours ago he'd been dressed in tailored trousers and a business shirt but he'd changed. He was now wearing faded jeans and a T-shirt that looked a bit too tight, revealing a pretty impressive six-pack. He was long, lean and tanned. His dark hair had lost the neatness she'd seen back at the hospital—maybe he'd just had a shower as it looked damp and a bit…rumpled.

He was smiling a greeting and the sight of him…

Post Harvey, she'd sworn off men for life. Independence was everything. More than any nun entering a convent, her vows had been real and meant—but surely the sight of this guy was enough to make even a good nun blink.

Oh, for heaven's sake, was she blushing? Get a grip, she told herself fiercely. She was here with a serious proposition. Emotion—and hormones—had to disappear.

She leaned into the back of the car to grab the parcel of fish and chips, which gave her time to regain her composure. Meanwhile, Boris had launched himself out to greet his new best friend—the world was composed of Boris's new best friends! When she turned, Rab had crouched to greet him, sending Boris into spasms of squirming ecstasy by rubbing behind his ears.

'Have he and I met in a previous life?' he asked, smiling as he rose, and she managed a grin.

'Not as far as I'm aware. Meet Boris.'

'Not into social distancing then, your Boris?'

'You could say that.' Then the big dog swivelled. A rabbit had peeped out from under the hedge at the edge of the driveway and Boris was off, baying as if the hounds of hell were after him.

'He'll never catch it,' she told him.

'Will he come home?'

'Are you kidding? He's been smelling fish and chips since town.'

He smiled again. 'Would you like to come inside?'

'The veranda's good.' Boris might not appreciate the niceties of social distancing, but for Mia social distancing—any sort of distancing— seemed imperative.

'Right.' So they sat on the top step with the parcel between them. Rab had gone inside and come out with two glasses of water.

'I should have wine,' he apologised.

'Water's great. Much safer for what we need to talk about.'

'What do we need to talk about?'

There was an interruption then as Boris tore back—had he heard the rustle of paper opening from the other end of the paddock? Moves had to be made to protect their dinner—which involved Mia carrying a large fish fillet down into the garden, offering it to Boris and then saying, 'That's it!'

And Boris got it. He looked adoringly up at her, wolfed the fish and then headed back to the hunt.

She returned to the steps, and Rab watched her come.

'This is surely one of the strangest dates I've ever had,' he told her, and she shook her head.

'It's not a date. It's a business proposition.'

'Then why aren't we in a lawyer's office?'

Maybe they should be, she thought. Maybe she shouldn't be wearing jeans and a faded sweatshirt, watching her dog hunt rabbits while she ate fish and chips. And the lawyer thing—that seemed deeply scary.

But it had to be faced, she told herself, and made herself say, 'That'll come, if you agree.'

'So what, exactly, would we be agreeing to?'

She met his gaze and held it for a long moment, and then turned her attention back to the fish and chips. She needed to take her time, get her words right. This was too important to mess up.

Right. Say it.

So she did, trying to get it out as quickly as possible.

'So,' she said, trying not to stumble over her words, 'I talked to Eric's mum. Eric's the kid who asked if you were married at the meeting. His mum's read the whole will, and I think… I think it might work. If you were agreeable…if you really wanted it…we could marry. But…just for twelve months. The ceremony would need to be legal, done properly. Because of the "happily settled" clause, I gather I'd have to move in here. We'd need to be seen to be married. But this is a big place and it's not like the olden days, lawyers checking sheets to make sure… to make sure things were consummated. We'd be housemates, that's all. And it would only be for a year, just to keep the valley safe.' She was talking too fast, she knew she was, but she had to get it out.

'And the legal thing. We could each use our own lawyers, people who have nothing to do with your grandfather's legal team. We could draw up agreements that mean we have no hold whatsoever on each other, financially or otherwise. But…' She faltered then but it had to be said. 'But I'd have to trust you not…not to sell the valley for coal mining.'

There was a pause. A long one.

'How could you trust me?' he said at last.

'I hardly know,' she said honestly. 'The marriage thing—that wouldn't mean anything, and I wouldn't want or take anything from it. I could put that in writing for you to use at the end of the twelve months. The valley thing though… When the marriage is over the valley will be yours and I don't think there's any way I could stop you selling it. But I don't think… I can't think that you would?'

She tilted her chin then and managed to meet his look head-on. 'It's trust,' she told him. 'I'm not… I'm not very good at it, but you must be a good man. Surely?'

There was another silence, a long, stretched out pause where they went back to eating their fish and chips while kookaburras chortled for the last time for the night in the massive eucalypts along the river, where bullfrogs started croaking in the reeds alongside the tiny creek bed meandering down through a rock bed to join the main waterway.

And then, into the stillness, he said, 'Mia, this is huge. How could you possibly trust?'

'I don't know. I only know that somehow… I might.'

Another silence and then, 'Mia,' Rab said quietly into the dusk, 'what happened to you?'

'It's nothing to do…' She faltered.

'With me? I think it must be. You're asking me to marry you.' He turned so he could meet her gaze head-on. 'This involves so much trust on both sides that complete honesty has to be the way to go.'

'I can't… I hate…'

'I imagine you do hate talking about it,' he told her. 'But, Mia, what you're suggesting isn't something small. I'd have to move here for twelve months, leave my job, leave everything I know.'

'But you'd win. You've have so much…at the end of it. You'd own this valley. You could sell parts of it, just not for coal mining. Individual sales. There are local farmers renting now who'd love to buy their land. You could make a fortune and leave the valley safe.'

'But you'd walk away with nothing. I need to know why you'd do that.'

'I told you. I love this valley.'

'Yes, and I want to know why. And I also want to know why, when you're talking to me, I can see fear in your eyes. You're making this suggestion, but what I see in your face…it's like you're offering yourself up to the guillotine.'

She struggled with that, but finally she managed a smile. 'It's not quite as bad as that.'

He smiled back, but his eyes didn't leave hers. 'Honesty, Mia. Lay it on the line. Even if this is only for twelve months, I won't marry someone I don't know. I think I have vague memories of you back at Sydney Central, as a burns patient, but I can't remember your history. I was an intern, not responsible for your care, only seeing you at night under bandages. I won't even consider this crazy proposition without openness on both our parts. Spill.'

* * *

Spill. Tell him the whole story?

Hardly anyone knew, at least not the whole story. A drunken partner, a fight, burns. That was pretty much what she told everyone now. It was only the social workers all those years ago—Robyn, and then Ewan and his wife, Mary, who knew it all.

This man was asking for everything. It felt like exposing herself to more pain to talk about it. But there was no choice. She'd decided to trust him enough to ask him to marry her. Maybe it was fair that he'd asked her to trust him more.

'It's a horrid story,' she said, determined to get it over fast. 'My father was a small-time drug grower and dealer, and he was damaged by the drugs he used. My mum, well, she was a bit of a doormat. She loved my dad—or maybe she didn't, it was just that she didn't have the courage or strength to leave. We lived on a sort of farm about ten kilometres north of Corduna. You don't know it? I'm not surprised, hardly anyone does. It's all red sand, rocks, thistles, the remains of opal mining, a community that's pretty much surviving on memories. We had a scraggy piece of land that was useless for growing anything but…but what we grew. But we didn't even own that—it belonged to a guy called Harvey Manton.

'Harvey lived in a huge house at the bottom of the district's only hill, with a succession of gorgeous girlfriends he imported from Sydney. His place was weird but it was his palace, a place where he had total control. He loved it. I made enquiries after...well, a long time after, and I bet it's still his. It was sold when he went to jail but one of his mates bought it, and I'm betting he'll end up back there. It was his own private kingdom. It had dogs, barbed wire, huge gates, floodlights and he was so proud of it. I sometimes think that most of his vitriol towards me in the trial was because what he did to me finally caused the authorities to breach his defences.'

She paused then, staring at nothing. Then shrugged and forced herself to go on.

'Anyway, most of the stuff Dad grew made money for Harvey. He was...he *was* big and mesmerising and violent, and...and Mum and Dad did everything he wanted. Then, when I was sixteen Dad got deeply in debt—or more deeply into debt—and Harvey decided he wanted me.'

He frowned, trying to get a grip on her story. 'Did you have brothers or sisters? Were there people around?'

'No. You need to understand—what Dad was growing was for Harvey, and isolation was everything. So there was just me and Mum. I used to go to school a bit, but it was a fifteen-minute drive into Corduna and then an hour by bus to the nearest town that had a school. There was always a reason why I couldn't go. In the end they enrolled me for home schooling to keep the authorities happy, but that was a joke. I used to read, though, a lot. Corduna had a library van that came most Fridays, and the librarian was kind, letting me borrow heaps in case I couldn't get there the next week. So I suppose I educated myself. As I got older I thought of running away but there was always Mum. Mum had appalling asthma and was always sick. I couldn't leave her. But then, when Harvey wanted me...'

She closed her eyes as the nightmare flooded back, then forced herself to go on. 'Well, Mum didn't have the strength to fight him, and in the end I couldn't either. So I agreed. He even said he'd marry me, and we ended up in a sort of pseudo marriage. When I was seventeen! Totally illegal, but I didn't know it. Harvey used to go away for long periods. I knew there were other women—but I was his.'

'Oh, Mia.'

She shrugged. 'It was just...what was. I've gone over and over it in my mind—and with the psychologists at the hospital before the court case. I accept there was nothing I could have done, not at that age. I was raised to fear him and that's what I did. And then, one day when I was nineteen, I didn't heat the oil enough when I cooked his chips. He was drunk, his chips were soggy, and he threw the oil at me. And that was sort of…that. Somehow I got myself back to Mum and Dad's. Mum was really sick by then, but when she saw me she got me into the car and drove me to the hospital. Even then Dad was yelling at her not to do it. But she did, and then there were police, social workers, you name it. They put Mum in hospital too, and Harvey went to jail.'

He looked as if he felt ill, appalled by the simple story. 'So…did you have support afterwards? Your mum?'

'Mum died before I finished rehab,' she said flatly. 'Emphysema as well as asthma. Dad did a twelve-month jail stint and then disappeared. I don't know where he is, and I don't care. And Harvey's still in jail. He's due to get out soon but I can't worry about that either.' Again a shrug.

'Anyway, the social workers at Sydney Central were wonderful, and one of them was Robyn, Ewan's daughter. She lived here as a kid. She and I… Well, she's supposed to keep her professional life separate, but rehab took ages, and in the end she felt like…my friend. Finally she asked if I'd like to come here for a while after rehab, and her dad and mum—Ewan, that's Doc Ewan, and his wife, Mary—took me under their wing. I still can't believe their kindness. They supported me to train as a nurse. The whole valley did. So the rest is history.'

There was a long silence. Finally Rab lifted his hand and ran a finger down the outline of the graft across her cheek. Like a doctor's examination—only not. She sat without flinching, feeling the touch but not feeling…anything.

'You poor bloody kid.'

And that roused her. The story itself still made her feel ill, recounting it, remembering the awful passivity of being a total victim. But his touch, his sympathy…

She stood so quickly that the paper of remaining chips was knocked and fell between the slats of the veranda steps. She moved to stand before him, at the bottom of the steps so her eyes were level with his.

'I'm not a poor bloody kid,' she said, one syllable at a time. 'I might have been once upon a time, but I'm not that person any more. I told you my story only because I need you to see how much I owe Robyn and Ewan and Mary, how much I owe this valley. I'll do whatever it takes to keep it safe, but I'll do it on my terms. I'm in control, Rab Finlay. What I'm offering could be good for you—you stand to be very wealthy—but it's my decision, made as an adult. The terms are mine. No one has power over me any more. I'm not being coerced. This is my decision, so take it or leave it. And don't...don't touch me again.'

She was standing before him, her hands on her hips, defiant, angry, challenging. Her dark eyes flashed fire.

What she was proposing was preposterous. To marry someone he didn't know... He shouldn't even consider it, but this woman...her story...

He remembered his stint in the burns unit all those years ago. Three months, done as part of his training. He'd been appalled.

And those weeks on night duty... Unless there were admissions it had been a relatively quiet rotation, but he'd been needed because pain levels had to be constantly monitored. The patients with burns to their lower body had been the easiest to care for in the night because they could tell him, they could call out if their pain became unbearable. But those whose faces had been severely burned... They needed to be watched, their body movements interpreted, rising blood pressure or even a twitching hand or arm maybe denoting there was excruciating pain being borne under the bandages.

He'd hated being helpless in the face of such suffering. His reading during his supposed meal breaks had been a way of watching for those signs, but it had also made him feel as if he was doing at least something.

At least something...

What this woman was offering was far more than something. Marriage...

It could be just as she'd said, he told himself. A simple contract, a house sharing for a year.

Suddenly he was thinking of practicalities. He'd need to give up his job at Sydney Central for a year, maybe work in the hospital here. He'd miss his job, he'd miss his friends, his life. This place was almost the back of beyond. He'd been raised in the city and the thought of living in the country for a year didn't appeal one bit.

He didn't need the money this inheritance brought with it. He was wealthy enough in his own right. But it'd only be for a year.

And this woman—she'd be sharing the house with him for a year but, other than that, her life wouldn't change. She wouldn't be giving up anything.

Except...

Her gaze still met his, the challenge still there, and he thought back suddenly to those nights in the burns unit, of pain, of helplessness. Caused by a guy who had total control over her.

She was offering to marry a man she didn't know for no financial gain at all. To thank the valley that saved her.

He suddenly felt very, very small.

'Your name?' he asked slowly, a sliver of memory surfacing.

'Mia.' And then she hesitated. 'Maira. I was Maira... Maira Somebody. The social workers helped me change it. Harvey...he thought he owned me. I didn't want to be that person any more.'

'Are you still afraid of him?'

'I told you. He's in prison.'

'When's he due for release?'

'Soon,' she said shortly. 'But that's okay. He won't find me. My name's been changed for years and if...if I marry you then I get to change it again.' She tilted her chin. 'Not that that's a reason for me to marry. I told you, Rab, there's nothing in this for me.'

'I'd want there to be something.'

'Free board for a year then,' she said. 'I'm renting a tiny cottage near the hospital. The backyard's tiny. Boris would love to live here.'

Hearing his name, Boris ceased investigating the pellets of poo down by the fence—from kangaroos? Rabbits?—and came dashing up, only to discover chips had fallen between the steps. How had that escaped his notice? His huge head dived straight down, until all that was between them was the dog's massive rear, tail rotating like a chopper blade.

It should have made Rab smile. It didn't. His feelings of inadequacy were deepening by the moment.

He'd had a life of absolute privilege. Sure, he'd lacked parenting, but there'd been nannies to fill in the gaps, often good ones. He'd had an easy path into medical school, and his father's death had left him wealthy. He was in a profession he loved. He had great friends, a great life.

The knowledge that he'd missed out on inheriting Cockatoo Valley hadn't upset him— he'd had no idea he'd stood to inherit anyway. He'd come to give the locals the news that had little to do with him, then visit his grandfather's house to see if there were family mementoes, anything his kids—if he ever had kids—might like. And then walk away.

Being honest, he'd hardly thought of the ramifications of the sale of this land. He'd hardly thought of the community about to be destroyed.

Yet now... Here was this woman, to whom community seemed to mean everything. She'd been through so much and yet...she was offering to trust again.

He had no doubt that the idea of marriage, accepting that she'd need to live with a stranger for a year, must bring with it an appalling level of fear, subliminal if not overt. Yet here she was, asking for nothing for herself, asking only that he marry her and live with her for a year, to save what she held so dear.

A year. Leaving Sydney. Living in this house. Suddenly he was taking the idea seriously.

He'd have to work, he thought. He wasn't born to be a country squire. But he'd been in the busy hospital, he'd seen the look of weariness on the elderly Ewan's face. That look surely wasn't solely caused by the thought of losing the valley. Ewan could use help.

So...could he work himself, here in this hospital? His role would be a family doctor instead of a surgeon at the top of his game. He'd have to brush up on a few things. Well, maybe more than a few, he thought ruefully. Diagnosis of minor ailments. What to do with nappy rash.

An overenthusiastic wiggle of Boris's behind pushed him sideways and he looked across the dog's massive backside and saw Mia watching him.

Calmly. Waiting for his verdict.

'I'll... I'll let you think about it,' she said. 'I have no right to ask it of you, so I'll accept whatever you decide. There's no blame on you.

This was your grandfather's doing, not yours.'
She shoved her hand between the steps and
grabbed Boris's collar. 'Come on, mate,' she
told him. 'Enough chips, we need to go home.
You know where to find me, Rab,' she told him.
'If...if you need me.' And she tugged.

But nothing happened. There were chips
down there. Mia was slight and Boris was seriously big. She tugged and tugged again.

And finally Rab grinned and shoved his hand
down with hers. A hand each on the collar, a
mutual tug and Boris emerged, his mouth full
of chips wrapping, his tail still whirling with
happiness.

And they stood for what seemed a loaded moment together, hands touching, dog wiggling
with delight between them.

The slight contact of hands. It seemed to
mean... What? Rab hardly knew. He only knew
that he didn't want to pull away.

'I... Thank you,' Mia said at last, and finally
their hands parted.

'Think nothing of it,' Rab told her. 'And I
have decided. Mia... If you'd do me the honour...' He gave a rueful grin. 'I should go down
on one knee, but it seems a mockery in the cir-
cumstances. Whatever, Mia, let's get married.'

CHAPTER FIVE

THE WEDDING TOOK place five weeks later. Four weeks was the legal minimum to lodge documentation of intention to marry, but it had taken a week to get that documentation sorted. Even then they were rushed, but a week before Rab's thirty-fifth birthday they stood before Cockatoo's local wedding celebrant and made their vows.

'Because there's no way I'm doing it in a church,' Mia had declared. 'I feel like I can cross my fingers behind my back when it's only Tony Gaylard, who thinks he's the king of everything around here. He's the shire president,' she'd explained to Rab. 'Retired accountant who does weddings and funerals as—he says—a public service. He's a pompous little man with bad taste in three-piece suits, and a huge notion of his own importance.'

Whatever, there was no doubting the delight of the little man who stood before them, taking them through their vows. He beamed as if all his Christmases had come at once.

As did Ewan and Mary, who stood behind them as witnesses. It was only their daughter Robyn, the social worker who'd introduced Mia to this valley, who was looking worried. She'd driven from Sydney because, as she'd told Mia, 'There's no way you're going into this without me being there.' Rab had thought it was an act of friendship, but the night before the wedding she'd driven out to Wiradjuri ready for an inquisition.

'Mum and Dad have told me all about you,' she'd said with no preamble. 'You sound like the answer to the valley's prayers, but I've cared about Mia for almost ten years and I'm not about to stop now. She's doing this for the valley, not for her, but I wish…oh, how I wish she could do something for herself. Anyway, I came here to tell you that if you hurt her…well, I can't tell you how many friends she has, in this valley and beyond. You'll take care of her or else.'

He had no idea of 'what else' implied, but he'd reassured her as best he could. Now she was standing beside her parents and the look of belligerence hadn't faded. Her arms were folded and she was looking straight at him with an air of pure judgement.

But he'd only glanced at her once. His attention was almost solely taken by Mia. His bride.

She'd dressed simply—no full bridal attire for this woman. The marriage was a business arrangement and that was what her clothes implied. A crisp white long-sleeved blouse with a high collar. Plain black trousers. Her hair was braided and coiled into a knot. She wore little make-up, her shoes were sensible—she looked as if she was about to head into a meeting with a bank manager.

Well, maybe that was pretty much what she was doing, he thought. She was making promises, signing documents that would ensure the financial security of this valley.

Her face was set—it hadn't changed from the moment he'd met her outside the council chambers. Oh, she'd given him a tight smile as he'd greeted her but that was all. Now she was staring straight ahead, making her vows mechanically, without expression.

Just how frightened was she? Her vows were sure and steady, but when he lifted her hand to put the ring on her finger he felt it trembling. She looked down at the ring and grimaced, just slightly, but the expression was fleeting. She went straight back to being stoic.

He had an almost overwhelming impulse to stop proceedings, to call a halt, to take her into an anteroom and make sure she hadn't changed her mind. What was he doing, marrying a woman who was terrified?

But the look on her face was transient, gone almost before he saw it. She glanced up at him and gave a decisive nod. *Do it*, her look said, and he slid the ring onto her finger. And then she put a ring on his finger because that was what they'd decided. For the next year they'd be a business partnership, equals. If she was to be married, then so was he.

'I now pronounce you man and wife,' the celebrant said, beaming as if this was the end of a fabled romance. 'You may kiss the bride.'

'You may kiss the bride.'

She remembered those words. She'd heard them years ago when, all of seventeen, she'd been standing before a man she'd been raised to believe was the centre of her family's universe. Harvey had controlled her father absolutely. His word was law, and her father obeyed him without question.

Mia's mother had done her best to efface herself when Harvey entered their house. Mia— Maira then—had also been taught from an early age to disappear when the men were at the kitchen table, drinking. She and her mother had mostly stayed in her bedroom, listening to

Harvey's voice booming out displeasure, orders, the way their life should be run.

Then, when she was thirteen, fourteen, Harvey had started watching her. He'd demanded that she stayed during his visits, that she poured his beer, that *she* served him instead of her frightened mother.

And then he'd decreed that she would marry him. And her father had explained how much of a hold the man had over them, that he'd go to jail if she didn't, and her mother too. It seemed they were all implicated.

The marriage had been a mockery. There'd been no documentation and she'd been too naïve to know it had been necessary. Even if it had been legal, she'd learned afterwards that there'd been another marriage that hadn't been dissolved.

But she'd had no choice. Her father was so deep in debt—and so deep into murkier dealings, things he was complicit in—that Harvey had total power. So she'd stood in a strange office, in front of a man the police had told her later was a 'mate', someone Harvey had bribed to say the words.

She'd been wearing her mother's old wedding dress, and they'd both been crying as they'd driven to the ceremony. She'd been a bride but not a bride, and when the pseudo-celebrant had said, 'You may kiss the bride,' Harvey had kissed her with a ruthlessness that held more than a promise of the cruelty to come.

'You're mine now,' he'd said, with an implacability that had made her terrified from that moment.

And now…here was another man standing beside her. They'd made the same vows, and those vows were also a mockery.

'You may kiss the bride.'

What was she doing? Putting herself in this man's power?

No, she told herself sharply. This was very different. It was her choice, her decision. She was the one with the control.

But was she kidding herself? Here she was, once again being asked to submit. *'You may kiss the bride.'* Code for: You may do whatever you want with this woman from now on—she's yours.

Rab was holding her hands, as bride and groom had done for centuries past as vows were made. He was ready to take this next step.

'You may kiss the bride.'

But maybe he saw her panic because, instead of kissing her, he started to speak.

'I think we need to change this,' he said softly, but loudly enough for everyone in the chamber to hear. 'Mia, you've married me, and I honour you for that. I honour the choice you've made, but choices don't stop with this ceremony. Mia, if you wish, and only if you wish… If you wish, you may now kiss the groom.'

There was a shocked hush in the tiny council chamber. Mia looked up into Rab's face and what she saw there…

No pressure, his expression said. *Take all the time you want. Or if you decide not to then it's fine, there'll be no kiss at all.*

She looked around almost wildly, tossed right out of kilter, and she saw Robyn, the social worker who'd been there for her almost from the beginning. Robyn, who had the reputation of being an attack dog where her clients were concerned. And Robyn was grinning. Grinning! Such a thing was almost unheard of.

And suddenly Mia found herself smiling back.

'*Mia, if you wish…you may now kiss the groom.*'

It was such a simple statement, but with it came an implicit promise. She might be doing this, but she wasn't losing control.

And she was suddenly thinking of this man's kindness from years ago, and that she'd had to talk him into marrying her. And, what was more, that he was doing so to save the whole valley.

So why not?

'Why not indeed?' she whispered, and she raised herself on tiptoes.

And she kissed him.

It was a feather kiss. A brush of lips, the merest touch. It was part of what was essentially a business deal. It shouldn't have meant anything to Rab at all.

Except when her hold on his hands tightened, when she raised herself a little on her toes, when she turned her face up to his, something twisted inside him.

Something he didn't understand at all.

CHAPTER SIX

THE WEDDING HAD been held in the early afternoon. The service itself was private but what happened afterwards was definitely not.

'Almost all the locals know why we're getting married,' Mia had told him. 'This is…well, it doesn't seem *our* marriage, Rab. It's more a community service.'

'Like the bob-a-job I used to do as a Boy Scout,' he'd joked, and then he'd had to explain the concept of kids doing odd jobs to raise money for charity.

'Exactly,' she'd agreed, and then thought about it. 'Or sort of. How much is a bob, exactly? Possibly a bit less than you'll be giving the valley.'

'But not as much as what you're giving,' he'd said, and she'd smiled but it had been that strained smile he was starting to know. The smile that said fear was still in the background.

'I'm not giving anything,' she'd told him.

'I'm gaining free rent for a year, for me and for Boris, but you're having to change your life.'

He was. He'd gone back to Sydney to quit his job, to pack up his apartment, to figure the minutiae of transferring his life to Cockatoo Valley for a year. He'd had to resign completely, give up the lease on his apartment, tell friends and colleagues he was leaving for good, because the terms of the will stated 'happily settled' and simply taking a year's absence wouldn't cut it.

'What are you doing?' his friends had demanded incredulously, and he'd asked himself pretty much the same question. But, increasingly, he had the answer.

It had cost him more than a pang to leave his hospital job, but there was an inheritance at the end of it. That was what he told himself—and his friends—and it made sense. But, added to that, there was also an element of…well, adventure was the wrong word but the thought of settling in the country, of doing something worthwhile, felt okay. More than okay, he decided as the wedding had approached and the ramifications for the locals became clearer. Often over the past years—maybe since he and Annabel had conceded their relationship wasn't working—he'd endured the unpleasant sensation that he'd been…drifting. Working in the valley for a year, helping out and in the process keeping this land safe for future generation—the prospect felt worthwhile. Even good.

And now, seeing Mia's face the night before the wedding, he'd thought she was giving up so much more. She was supposedly in control. She'd been the instigator, but in the end what was in this for her but another arranged marriage?

She was determined though. She was doing it for the community, she'd see it through, and practically the whole community knew it. So the ceremony itself was private, but the moment they emerged as man and wife they were ushered into the hall next door, where the party to end all parties had been set up. The future of the valley had been secured by this marriage, and the locals were intent on celebrating in full.

But Mia wasn't celebrating. As the afternoon wore on, as Rab received congratulations and thanks, followed by congratulations and thanks, until his face ached from smiling in response, he saw the rigidity behind Mia's smile and wondered again at the personal cost of her decision.

She looked exhausted. How long did they have to stay there? But it was up to Mia, he thought. This was her community, it had to be her call.

In the end it was Robyn who saved them. Robyn was a big-bosomed, big-hearted woman, and Rab could imagine her years ago, taking the shattered Mia under her wing and bossing her parents to take care of her. Even though she lived and worked in Sydney, she apparently still thought of the valley as home, and when her parents had told her what Mia and Rab had arranged she'd arrived back in the valley within hours. And cornered Rab.

'I hate that Mia's doing this,' she'd said flatly. 'But she's doing it for all of us. It's her decision and I need to accept it. But she's told you her background? In my opinion she's still totally vulnerable, and if you hurt her, I swear, I'll trash your reputation from here to Timbuctoo. You might have a great name as a general surgeon, but I'm pretty high up in the social services network and I can make it happen.'

But then she'd thrown herself into organisation mode. She, with her father, had been witness to their marriage, and now she made her way through the crowd to corner bride and groom.

'Enough,' she told them. 'It's six already, but this party looks like going until midnight. The whole valley's ecstatic but you guys must be bushed. And I bet you haven't eaten. There's more food here than you can shake a stick at, but you've been talked at all the time. So we've packed a hamper and my kids have taken it down to the riverbank at the bottom of your garden. They've set up a picnic for you, everything you need. Dad'll make a speech now, and then you can make a getaway.'

So they listened as Ewan made an emotional speech saying how much this marriage meant to them all. The whole community cheered and Rab took his bride's hand and led her out of the hall. They drove away—with tin cans and old boots trailing from the car behind them.

It had been a typical country wedding. Sort of.

Mia seemed almost mute.

They reached the house—their house—and the silence seemed to intensify.

'Where's Boris?' Rab asked as they climbed from the car. He hadn't thought of the dog, but he thought now that Boris should be here. Mia needed something to take that look from her face. The fiercely independent woman who'd proposed to him was suddenly nowhere. She was afraid?

What should he say? He thought for a moment and then ventured, 'Right, let's start as we mean to go on. Marriage in name only, as we've agreed. We're housemates, Mia, nothing more. So right now we don't need to use Robyn's picnic basket. If you like, you can go to your end of the house and I'll go to mine. Rostered time for kitchen and bathroom use? Do you want to make yourself a meal first? I know Robyn's filled the fridge so we can commence independent living—starting now?'

And, blessedly, the strained look eased from Mia's face. She even managed a smile.

'It does seem a waste,' she conceded. 'Maybe... friends might picnic?'

'So we might. But where's Boris?'

'Robyn's taken him for the night. He needs a decent run and I wouldn't... I didn't think I'd have time. She has four kids who'll oblige.'

'Do you want him back? We could go fetch him if you like.' He hesitated. 'I'm not too tired to walk him—or you could walk him if you're up to it.'

'The kids'll be disappointed if we do that,' she told him, seemingly moving on from discussing independence. 'And so will Boris. Robyn gave him to me as a puppy, and her kids think of him as part theirs.'

'Robyn's been a good friend.'

'She's been my lifesaver,' she said, and he heard the depth of emotion behind her words. 'Between your reading *The Wind in the Willows* and her friendship...' Her voice wobbled but then she smiled again. 'So, moving on... Maybe independent dinner tonight is silly—we can hardly leave Robyn's picnic hamper down at the river. And I'm hungry enough to eat a horse. We can split the picnic hamper down the middle if you like, and maybe turn our backs on each other, but it does seem a bit ridiculous. Between…friends?'

And her voice faltered again as she said the last word. It was a question.

A hope?

He met her eyes. They were wide and strained. He could see dark shadows, and he wondered how much she'd slept the night before. Or any time in the last few weeks.

What a leap of faith this had been. What a measure of trust.

'Definitely friends,' he told her, smiling down into her eyes. Hoping she might smile back. 'Give me five minutes to get out of this damned suit and let's go share.'

It was a good thing to do. In casual clothes, jeans and T-shirt on his part, jeans and an over-sized shirt tied at the waist on hers, they headed down to the sandy 'beach' formed by a curve in the river. There they found a picnic rug, two canvas deckchairs, a mountain of cushions and an enormous picnic hamper. A romantic wedding feast.

They opened the hamper and were both astounded.

This hadn't been made by scouring the hall

for leftovers, Rab thought. It was almost… Robyn's wedding gift to them. Had she brought it from Sydney, guessing how much they'd need to get away?

Regardless, it was amazing. There was lobster meat and prawns, nestled on a a crisp salad complete with with silver salad servers and slivers of lime and lemon. There were delicate sandwiches with exotic fillings. There were profiteroles stuffed with salmon and a creamy dressing to die for. Olives, pastrami, oozy French Camembert, wafer-thin crackers…

Then tiny meringues, with cream in one bowl, strawberries, raspberries and blackberries in another, plus a jar of homemade lemon curd so they could make their own tiny pavlovas.

And beside the hamper there was champagne in an ice bucket—the best. There was a note tied to the champagne: 'Happy Wedding from the entire valley'.

Mia read the note and her eyes shimmered. Even Rab felt… Well, guys surely didn't do shimmering, but it was a close thing. In the last few weeks he'd realised just how momentous this marriage was for the whole valley. How much Mia had given them.

Now he looked at Mia and he made a silent vow—a vow much more meaningful than any of the fake wedding vows they'd just made. This would not hurt her and he wouldn't let her be hurt. Ever. He'd seen her fear back at the house. For her to suggest this, to make yet another arranged marriage…

'We've done a good thing,' he said, and she managed a wavery smile.

'I…yes. Thank you. I can't tell you…'

'Then don't. There's no need for you to thank me. The privilege is all mine. Yes, you get free rent for a year but I get a year off from a high-pressure job, I get to share a house with an amazing woman, with a great community, and at the end I inherit a fortune.'

'But you won't sell.' He heard the flash of fear and he got it. Even now, she was still frightened for her beloved valley.

'I won't sell,' he told her. And then he grinned. 'You know, when I was talking to my lawyer about this marriage I was reminded that if we live together as man and wife for two years then half of what's mine is yours anyway. That's the law. So you just need to stick with me for an extra twelve months and the valley's yours anyway.'

'Oh, my…' She stared at him in horror. 'But I wouldn't. Rab, I swear I wouldn't. I'll be moving out the day our twelve months is up.'

His smile widened. 'Hey, it's okay, Mia, I'm not sweating on losing anything—and it'll be me who'll be moving. Meanwhile, I can't remember a double shift in our Emergency Department coming even close to today for building an appetite, and here we have a feast fit for royalty. So...'

He popped the champagne cork, filled two glasses and handed one to her. 'Here's to our version of happy ever after,' he told her, clinking their glasses. 'Here's to happy for twelve months, after which all problems will be sorted. And here's to one brave woman, who has the courage to trust.' His gaze met hers and held. 'Here's to you, Mia. Well done.'

They ate and drank in silence, leaning back on the mass of cushions. They'd have to lug them up to the house afterwards, Mia thought, because otherwise they'd end up covered in possum or kangaroo poo as the wild creatures of the night investigated. But right now it didn't seem to matter. Nothing mattered except the thing was done.

The valley was safe.

She was eating dinner with...her husband.

The word was enough to make her shiver, but the peace of this place, Rab's silence, the magnificence of the food, the luscious champagne—they were almost enough to keep the fears of the last few weeks at bay.

She could trust this man...couldn't she?

She had to. She had no choice.

And that brought a jarring note. No choice? Wasn't this where she'd come in before? Accepting a marriage because she'd had no choice.

The thought broke through the haze brought on by fatigue, good food, great champagne, the comfort of these cushions, the rug, this man's smile... Here it was again, washing back as if it was a part of her, as maybe it was. The eternal fear. It made her shudder and Rab's hand was suddenly touching her arm.

'Hey,' he said. 'It's okay, Mia. Your plan's worked brilliantly. All is good.'

Did he realise? Of course he did, she thought. He'd seen her as she'd been all those years ago. He hadn't remembered her in particular—well, who could? She'd been swathed in bandages, swollen beyond recognition. But even if he didn't recognise her, he'd worked with other burn patients. He'd know the damage.

He'd understand the fear.

'Is this river safe for swimming?' he asked, and she had to jerk herself out of thoughts that were messing with her head and focus on the here and now. River. Safe?

'It is at the moment,' she managed. 'Wide, sandy bottom, not too deep. I swim a lot, but further downstream. There's the occasional fallen branches so you need to be a bit cautious, and after heavy rains it's treacherous, but we've had no storms recently and the current's slow. It'll be safe enough. Cold though.'

'It's just what I need to wake me up,' he told her, rising. 'You want to come in too?'

'No. Thank you.' Swimming was one of her principal pleasures, but she hadn't swum where anyone could see her since burns had scarred the left side of her body as well as her face. She wouldn't say that, though. 'I'm too tired to swim,' she said, and she said it a bit too brusquely.

But he didn't appear to mind. 'Fair enough,' he said and put his head to one side to look at her. His dark eyes twinkled with mischief. 'But I'm not so tired. Would you be shocked if I stripped to my boxers and dived in? Or could I ask you to close your eyes?'

That smile was impossible to resist. He was looking down at her almost as if he was daring her to laugh as well, and to her astonishment she found her lips twitching, her mood lightening.

'I'm your wife,' she said, making her voice prim. 'I believe there's a legal prerogative for seeing you…'

'Just in boxers. Not the rest.'

'Of course,' she said, still primly. 'As per the conditions of our contract. But I'm a nurse.

There's nothing you can show me I haven't seen a thousand times before. Off you go and have fun.'

'You sound like a parent giving her kid permission.'

'Nope,' she told him. 'I have no control over what you do, but I will act as lifesaver.'

'So if a crocodile appears...'

'There aren't a lot of crocodiles in inland New South Wales,' she told him. 'But there may be eels. If any eel wanders by, can you grab it? I hate them—have you ever tried cooking an eel?—but Boris loves them.'

'So I'm heading in looking for dog food.'

'You might as well make yourself useful,' she told him serenely. 'Me, I'm going to make myself another pavlova.'

Except she didn't. She sat and watched Rab.

He strode into the water with confidence and plunged straight in, but he was obviously aware of the dangers of swimming in inland rivers. Instead of swimming, he floated out, presumably using his legs to check for depth, for underwater snags. What he found seemed to reassure him because he then began to swim. Not fast but strongly, his deep, sure strokes taking him from one end of the river's curve to the other.

As promised, he'd stripped to his boxers. He

looked superbly fit, lean and muscled, power-ing through the water with ease. He looked like a man completely at home in his environment.

At home. The phrase seemed to slam into her head. He was at home and so was she. For a year.

Another wave of panic swept over her, but she suppressed it with what was starting now to seem accustomed effort. Every time she thought of this marriage the old feelings of fear surfaced again, and every time she managed to damp them down.

The thing was done. For better or worse...

Rab rolled over and started to do a lazy backstroke. His body glistened, the light from the sinking sun glinting on his wet chest. He glanced over at her and grinned.

'It's magic. You sure you don't want to come in?'

'I'm sure.' There was that flutter of panic again, the thought of stripping—to what, bra and knickers? The thought of being in the water with him. The thought of being close, of not being in charge...

She had to keep control. Whatever happened over the next twelve months, she had to stay apart.

There'd been a moment during those awful months as her parents had bullied and cajoled her into marrying Harvey, when she'd looked at Harvey and thought maybe it wouldn't be so bad. He'd been big, burly, tough, but he had been good-looking. He used to smile at her, and sometimes she'd found herself smiling back. At seventeen she'd even found herself fantasising...

Yeah, well, she wasn't fantasising now.

Except she wanted, quite badly, to swim.

She knew a swimming hole a couple of kilometres to the north, where the river wound its way into bushland, a place no one seemed to use. She'd found it in those first months after Ewan and Mary had taken her in. She'd often swum there, tentatively at first but getting braver as she'd realised how private the place was. It had helped her head as well as her healing body, to swim where no one could see.

But here someone—Rab—would see.

Oh, but to swim... The sun was sinking to the west, its gorgeous tangerine rays shimmering along the river. Rab was doing lazy backstroke, not even watching her.

Dammit, why not? What sort of coward was she? This man was a doctor. He'd seen her maybe at her worst. What was there to fear?

'Just the way he makes me feel,' she muttered to herself, but that was dumb. Why shouldn't she swim?

Do it.

And thirty seconds later she'd ditched her shoes, jeans and shirt and she'd dived straight in.

Fear, after all, was just plain stupid.

He was backstroking steadily along the far side of the riverbank. He saw her dive and he stopped, let his feet fall to the sandy bank, watching as she surfaced.

She found her feet, glanced at him and he saw her chin tilt, almost as in defiance.

'I can swim even if I'm tired.'

'So you can,' he said, grinning. 'Amazing. Wonder Woman Plus!'

'There's no need to sound patronising.'

'I didn't!'

'Yes, you did. And it's unwarranted. I reckon I might even be able to swim faster than you. Four laps, along to the bend and back, repeated. Ready, set, go.'

And she was off, her body slicing through the water like a dolphin.

He watched her go, stunned. This wasn't the Mia he thought he knew. This was a woman of strength, of power. She was sleek, toned…gorgeous.

He could see scars on her upper shoulder, visible when she lifted her left arm. They didn't make her one whit less beautiful.

She reached the bend, did a flip turn, then saw he wasn't following. She found her feet in the breast-deep water and glowered. 'What?'

'What do you mean, what?'

'What are you staring at?'

'You.'

'Then don't,' she said brusquely and almost instinctively hugged her left arm with her right hand so the worst of the scarring was hidden.

'I wasn't staring at the scars. I was watching you. Mia, you're beautiful.

She glowered. 'I'm not beautiful. That's a dumb thing to say. You're just trying to avoid the question as to whether you're faster or me. Aren't you going to race?'

'We are racing,' he said, because he couldn't think what else to say. 'I just missed the gun. Starting now!' And he dived back under and started swimming.

He didn't make the mistake of trying to swim slower than she did. He swam the hardest he could, back and forth, back and forth. He was pushing himself to the limit but, even so, barely keeping up with her.

And the image of her stayed with him as he swam. It wasn't just the image, he decided, it was the consciousness of her. The thought that she was in the water beside him. That she was swimming with him, stroke for stroke.

Her long black hair, coiled for the wedding, had come undone. It was streaming behind her as she swam. He shouldn't even know that, but of course he did. He could see her every time he lifted his head and looked to the side.

She was his wife. It was a dumb thought, an extraordinary make-believe concept, but it stayed with him.

But she wasn't his. She was in control, she belonged to no one. If he didn't accept that then he should never have married her.

Still, he was in one of the most beautiful places in the world, and Mia was swimming beside him. The sense of her presence made him feel… Hell, he didn't know how it made him feel. Magic?

He couldn't examine the feeling. All he could do was keep on swimming.

It was Mia who finished first—of course it was. She did her four laps and she beat him. Then she pulled herself up on the grassy bank, grabbed her gear and headed for the bushes surrounding the clearing.

When she returned, Rab was just emerging

from the river, and even though she was dressed again, even though there'd been nothing in the fact that they'd swum together that had altered their relationship, she felt...exposed. It was a dumb sensation, but she couldn't help what she was feeling. What lay between them was too raw, too new, too ridiculous! Confused, she headed across to the picnic hamper, knelt and started packing up.

When she finally looked up, Rab was standing less than a metre away. His wet body was glistening in the last rays of the sun. His hair, naturally wavy, was soaked but still trying to kink. He'd snagged his shirt on one of the bushes and was starting to dry himself with it, but he was smiling right at her.

'That was awesome,' he said gently. 'You're an amazing swimmer, Mia.'

'Nope,' she said, a bit too abruptly. 'I'm not. I never swim in public.'

'Because of your scars?'

'I... No.'

'It'd be a shame if that was the reason,' he told her. 'If you have the courage to marry me, then maybe you could find the courage to swim wherever you want.' His smile changed then, subtly, and suddenly he sounded infinitely kind. Like the doctor he was. 'Mia, you're beautiful,' he told her. 'And you're beautiful from the inside out. Don't let that bastard control you any more.'

She flinched, closed her eyes, felt a wash of grief. But not fear. What was it with this man's voice? Right from that first time, when he'd read to her, it had settled something deep within. Pushed the fear away.

'I might,' she managed. 'Eventually.'

'There's no reason to wait,' he said, his voice still gentle. 'Now's beautiful. Grab the moment.'

She rose. He put a hand out to help her but she didn't take it. She didn't dare.

He was too close. Too wet. Too… Rab.

'I'll take the leftovers up to the house,' she said, a bit too quickly.

'Of course.' The moment was over; he was starting to dress. 'It's time for this day to end. It's been momentous.'

'In a way,' she told him. 'But…you have to remember the marriage means nothing.'

'It saved this valley,' he told her. 'I think it means everything.'

But not personally, she thought as she folded the picnic rug. I might be married but nothing's changed for me.

Was she lying, even to herself?

And then her thoughts were interrupted as a cry rang out from somewhere around the bend in the river. The cry sounded so terrified that her eyes swung to Rab's in instinctive alarm.

'Trouble,' he said.

Trouble—here in paradise?

Whatever, Rab tugged on his shoes, grabbed her hand and they started to run.

CHAPTER SEVEN

IT WAS THE BLACKBERRIES. And kids.

Wiradjuri had been built on a curve of the river. Although the Finlays owned all the land, most of it was leased. The land around the house had been fenced off—a hectare or so kept for gardens—but outside the boundaries was farmland.

But just around the bend, before garden became leased land, a massive clump of blackberry briars grew by the river, clumping out around the trees overhanging the water.

These were the berries Nora had talked of the first time Rab had seen the place. What had she said? A noxious weed, but his grandfather had loved the fruit. He knew them for a problem. The fruit from wild blackberries was delicious, but if left to spread they could envelop the countryside. He'd meant to ask her to get rid of them regardless, but these last weeks had been... Well, there'd been other things on his mind.

And now he and Mia rounded the bend and saw disaster.

A group of three kids, ranging from what looked like around thirteen down to about ten, had obviously been collecting berries. They had buckets set up beside the briars. There was a dog with them, and he recognised him—Boris! Dog and kids were all staring out over the river, and the little girl was screaming.

'Get out! Harry, get out! Harry, you'll hurt yourself...'

What was happening? They were all staring out over the water.

The briars had clumped as they'd grown out, extending almost halfway across the river. The berries above the water looked massive, black, shiny and almost untouchable.

'Help me!' It was another muffled cry, coming from the centre of the briars hanging over the water. It wasn't nearly as loud as the cry from the child on the bank, but it held more terror. And pain. And, even before they reached them, Rab could guess what had happened.

The kids looked like they'd been swimming—wet hair, damp clothes, towels dumped on the riverbank. They must have had a swim and then decided to pick blackberries before going home.

A massive eucalypt grew right near the bank,

and one of its branches reached out over the water. Vast, low, the limb hung enticingly above a massive clump of unpicked fruit.

And it seemed one child hadn't been able to resist. He—Harry—must have crawled out along the branch. And then slipped?

The briars were a little more than a metre below the branch, a great clump supported—sort of—by smaller bushes that had grown out over the water. A bucket lay incongruously on its side, resting on the top of the blackberry clump.

They couldn't see the child, but they had the picture. If he'd climbed out on the branch and slipped, his weight would have seen him slip into the centre of the briars. If he'd gone right through he would have ended up in the water, but the briars were thick, twined with age, impenetrable. They were strong enough to hold a child fast.

They were too strong to let a child out of their thorny grasp.

What the…? How on earth to get a child out of this?

'They're Robyn's kids,' Mia breathed, sounding horrified. 'They'll have brought our picnic and stayed.'

'Tell me about Harry,' he snapped. He needed information fast, and she understood.

'Fifteen. Good kid, responsible. Robyn would be trusting him to take care of the younger ones.'

Rab stared out over the water, his brain in overdrive, while Mia headed to the group of kids on the bank. The littlest, the only girl, melted into her arms with a shattering sob. Boris attempted to get in on the cuddle, and the two boys melted into the mix as well. It seemed Mia was known, was trusted. The relief of the group at her arrival was obvious.

'It's okay, we're here now,' Mia said, pulling back. The hugs had been necessary, but they had to move past it. 'That's Harry stuck in the bushes? Yes? Is it only Harry?'

'Yes,' one of the boys answered, turning to stare at the point where Harry had obviously disappeared. 'Mum... Mum and Dad are at the wedding and they said we could swim after bringing the picnic for you guys. Harry's got his lifesaving medallion, and all of us can swim. But we all love blackberries and Mum loves making jam, so we thought we'd bring buckets and surprise her. Will he fall out into the water? It's okay, he can swim really well.'

A child falling into the water was the least of their problems, Rab thought. A child trapped in those thorny briars was far more serious. If he struggled, these thorns were sharp enough to cut him so severely he'd…

Don't go there.

'Harry!' He raised his voice to pretty much sonic boom level. 'This is Dr Finlay. I'm here with Mia, and we're coming to get you out. But for now we need you to stay absolutely still. You're safe as long as you don't move.'

'They're sticking into me,' a terrified voice wailed. 'I'm bleeding. It hurts. I can't… I can't get out.'

'I know that,' Rab called. 'But if you move it'll be worse.'

'Harry, we're here,' Mia called out, adding her voice to Rab's. 'We're going to get you out, but you need to do what Dr Finlay says. It might take a little time to get to you though, so you have to stay still.'

'We need the fire brigade,' Rab snapped. 'Big ladders.'

'We don't have a fire brigade here,' she told him. 'Nearest is Colambool, an hour away.'

'Okay, then.' He moved on. 'Plan. You stay here and watch like a hawk. Talk to him all the time. Keep telling him he mustn't move. Can you contact his parents? Tell them where we are? Then contact anyone else with ladders, domestic ones—we can put 'em together if we must. Ropes too.'

'It'll take too long,' she said faintly. 'And I don't have my phone. Do you...?'

'You can use my phone, but I won't have stored numbers for anyone local.' He hauled it out of his pocket and tossed it to her. 'Security pin's seven-six-nine-six. Got that?'

She caught it easily. 'Seven-six-nine-six. Got it.' She took a deep breath and suddenly he was reminded of colleagues, fellow medics standing in Emergency, waiting for the arrival of trauma victims. From a shocked bystander, she was suddenly professional. 'I know enough numbers. I'll ring the hospital,' she said briskly.

She was still holding the little girl close but her voice was clipped and sure. 'They need to be put on notice anyway, and they'll contact the hall, get the help we need. Are you going to get a ladder?'

'Even if I find it, one's useless and it'll take too much time to get up to the house and back. Okay, kids... Can you tell me your names?'

'Mack and Wally,' the older boy said. 'And Louise. I'm Mack.'

'Right, Mack and Wally, we have gear we need just around the river bend and I need your help to carry it. Louise, you stay here and keep talking to Harry.' He called out again, 'Harry, we'll be with you in about ten minutes. Can you keep absolutely still for that long? Mia will talk to you all the time, but you must keep still. I know it's hurting but it'll hurt more if you move. Can you do that?'

There was a moment's silence and then, in a quavering voice, 'Yes.'

'Good man,' Rab called. 'What a hero. Okay, Mia, over to you.'

She had no idea what he intended. He was gone and all she could do was trust him.

Trust.

It was being stretched to the limit, she thought, but that was all this day had been about. Trust.

She needed him to save the valley. She needed him to save a kid's life.

And it was as critical as that, she thought. These briars were vicious and if Harry struggled, the cuts he inflicted could well cause enough blood loss to…

Don't go there. Just trust, she told herself, as Rab was asking Harry to trust.

They had no choice.

She crouched and held Louise close—the little girl was sobbing in a mixture of fear and fright—and she talked to Harry.

'Doc Finlay's on his way. He's a big city doctor, he knows exactly what to do, and Mack and Wally are helping. They've gone to get ropes to pull you out.' She had no idea what exactly he was getting, but ropes seemed the most reassuring thing to mention. 'And hey, the bucket you dropped on the briars is still upright. I don't reckon you've dropped a single berry. Your mum and dad will feel so proud.'

But also guilty? They'd only just started to trust Harry to take care of the littlies. Robyn would be beside herself.

Recriminations, though, were for the future. For now she called on, worrying that Harry's replies were getting fainter.

But then, faster than she'd thought possible, Rab and the boys were back. Between them they were carrying the two folded deckchairs, the picnic rug and their towels.

'Hey, Harry,' Rab called the moment he came within earshot. 'We're back with gear to get you out of there. Hang on, mate, we're coming.'

No answer. There'd been no answer for a couple of minutes now. Rab's voice was grim. 'Mia, how are you at climbing?'

'Good as a monkey,' she told him. 'Or maybe better. I do rock climbing in the hills up behind the town.'

'You're kidding me, right?' There was time for a flicker of astonishment. 'Well, hooray for Mia.'

'I could climb out…'

'And pull the kid up? How big is he?'

She thought of Harry, fifteen years old, a skinny adolescent but tall for his age. There was no room for false pride here. 'Too big for me. No.'

'Okay, then.' He looked totally focused on what lay ahead. 'You're backup. I'm heading out to just above where Harry is. I'll take the picnic rug. When I'm in position, Mia, I want you and Mack to climb out after me. Mia, you'll be closest to me. Mack, you'll stay close to the bank, not above the briars. When we're in position, Wally and Louise, I want you to hand the chairs to Mack, he'll hand them to Mia and she'll hand them to me. My plan is to throw the rug down onto the briars, then lower the folded deckchairs side by side onto the rug. It'll make a platform. Then I'll slide down, lie on the platform and pull Harry out.'

You're kidding, Mia thought. The whole thing might slip. And how was he going to pull Harry out? He'd surely have the strength, but his arms... But there was no choice and she knew it. The silence from Harry was an alarm all by itself.

Without thinking, she hauled open her shirt and tugged it off, handing it over. 'Put it on back to front,' she told him brusquely. 'It shouldn't mess with your climbing—even if it catches and rips it doesn't matter. When you're ready to reach into the briars, haul the sleeves down over your hands. It's not much protection but it's better than nothing.'

But suddenly Louise was stepping back, staring at Mia's side in horror. 'What's wrong with your middle?' she gasped. 'Yuk.'

'It's not yuk,' Rab said, before Mia could even think about responding. He was already hauling on her shirt. 'Those marks are like a medal for bravery. Some people get tattoos. Some indigenous Australians use scars to show they're grownup. These are scars that show Mia is a very special person, and here she is, doing something special all over again.' He shoved his hands into her shirtsleeves, tucked the flopping front into his pants and picked up the picnic rug. 'Right, let's get Operation Rescue Harry underway.'

What followed was breathtaking in the worst kind of way. Mia was finding it really, really hard to breathe.

Rab headed out onto the branch, inching his way out over the thick, smooth surface. 'I can see him,' he called and that was a relief in itself. 'I think I can get down to him.'

Then it was her turn to climb, inching out until she was on the branch a couple of metres back from Rab. Then Mack climbed into position.

She watched as Rab lowered the rug—thick, waterproof with a tartan wool top, blessedly sturdy—onto the briars. Then Wally and Louise lifted the first deckchair out to Mack. He managed to manoeuvre it to her and she passed it on to Rab. It sounded easy, but it wasn't. They did it, though, and once it was done, Rab lowered it with care onto one side of the blanket.

Then the other. The platform was formed.

Who needed to breathe? She watched, seemingly not breathing at all, as he lowered himself down. There was a moment of heart-stopping concern as he let go of the branch, but somehow he managed to balance, lowering his weight onto both chairs. Then he was lying face down, his body over the chairs, his face free to look down.

Would his makeshift platform hold? If he pulled the boy up, would their combined weight tip the chairs?

All she could do was keep holding her breath as he pushed his shirt-covered hands down through the briars.

'Grab,' she heard him say, then again, more roughly, 'Come on, Harry, you can do this. One big effort—grab.'

And then that terrifying wait, as slowly he hauled upwards, inching backwards on the platform as he tugged, as the boy emerged from the briars, as Rab gave one final tug. And finally the kid was free, and Rab was back on the platform, holding Harry tight, man and boy a combined heap entwined on the rigid chairs.

There was a long moment of silence, where Rab simply held, cradling the boy tight against him. Where human contact must surely be the most important thing.

Safe, Mia thought dazedly. Safe!

But then Rab was pulling back, just slightly, but far enough for her to see a wash of blood against his chest. He was hauling her shirt from his arms, then using it to form a pad, applying pressure.

'He might have nicked an artery,' he called curtly, speaking up to her, but then focusing again on the boy he was treating. 'It's okay, mate,' he told Harry. 'You're safe now. We've got you. Scratches all over and your arm's cut, but we can fix this. I'll just bandage your arm and then we'll lie still until your mum and dad come with ladders and ropes to get us down.'

'I want… Mum.'

'She's coming,' Mia said, loud enough to reassure Harry. Loud enough to reassure everyone. 'Joanne at the hospital has contacted the hall. I think we'll have everyone in Cockatoo Valley here, any minute now.'

* * *

It wasn't quite that soon. It was maybe fifteen minutes before the cavalry arrived, a convoy of cars, stopping at the property gates in the distance, then bumping their way over the paddocks.

And in their midst…a crane.

Mia was still lying on the branch. She couldn't do anything. She'd sent the boys back to the bank, but she couldn't bear to be where she could no longer get a clear view of Rab or Harry. She'd eased herself further out, so she was just above them.

'Joanne's sent the crane,' she told Rab. He was lying very still, holding Harry beside him, supporting his arm, keeping it high above his head. His shirt—*her* shirt—had been fashioned into a tourniquet and the bleeding had slowed but there were so many other scratches. She knew by Rab's face that blood pressure was a problem. Dear heaven, if Rab hadn't managed to get him out…

But he was out, and now good practical help was here. She'd told Joanne, the hospital night nurse, what the problem was and Joanne, from a farm herself, had thought things out and ordered accordingly.

In one of the first cars was Doc Ewan, with Mary and Robyn and her husband. They tumbled out of the car and the kids were enveloped in hugs in seconds.

The second vehicle to arrive was a small, sturdy truck and it was loaded with a stretcher—the good one, the one they kept for hauling rock-climbers down from the steep slopes around here when they came to grief. The one with straps, hand grips, everything they needed.

Then came ladders, ropes and people. The valley's farming community had arrived here in force. And Jeff Burrows had brought his crane, which was small, tough, pretty much a bucket of rust. Its almost sole use was pulling cows out of muddy bogs, which was a neat little side earner for Jeff when the locals didn't fancy spending big on hiring one of the fancier units from Co-lambool.

These people were mostly farmers, practical, resourceful, eager to help, and in what seemed seconds they had things organised. The crane was in position and the stretcher was being lowered, Mia using her spot on the branch to help stabilise it.

Then Rab, somehow stable enough on his platform to manoeuvre Harry onto the stretcher, was attaching him with straps. Then the stretcher was lifted and slowly swung back across the briars with the crane above holding it steady all the way.

Hands reached out to receive it, hauling it down to the riverbank, Ewan taking charge. 'You're all right, boy, we have you, here's your mum and dad.' Robyn was hugging her son, but sensible enough to keep his arm elevated.

Ladders were being positioned over the briars, many ladders, and the crane was used again, with a harness, so Rab had a handhold while he crawled back.

Meanwhile, people were helping her back, encouraging her until her feet touched solid ground. Rab reached the bank almost as she did, and grabbed one of the towels and wrapped her with it like a shawl. He was hiding the scars she'd hardly thought of, she realised, and she felt almost pathetically grateful. There wasn't time to say so, though—he was heading for Harry.

'I'm right, Rab,' Ewan said gruffly, glancing up from where he was kneeling over Harry's stretcher. Ewan might be elderly but there was no doubting his competence, and he was now the doctor in charge. 'We'll get an IV set up, get Harry into hospital and get these cuts seen to. But, Rab, you're scratched yourself. Mia, can you take care of him?'

'Of course,' she said, and suddenly her voice was shaky. Most of the blood on Rab was Harry's, but his hands... Her shirt hadn't stopped all the damage.

She glanced around at the crowd of people. There was so much help. These kids were in safe hands.

Neither of them was needed any more.

'We'll take Boris,' she told Robyn's husband, who was standing with his arms round as many of his kids that'd fit. They didn't need a spare dog tonight. 'Ewan, are you sure you're okay without us?'

'I'm sure,' Ewan said, glancing up from the stretcher. Apart from the night shift staff, practically every member of the Cockatoo Valley Hospital was right here. 'Go, you two. Thanks for saving my grandson, Rab. I can look after my family now. It's time you took your family home.'

They abandoned the picnic gear—the night creatures could have their way with what was left, they'd collect the rest in the morning. They walked slowly back to the house. Once Mia stumbled on the rough ground between garden and house and Rab took her hand. It was an unconscious action. There was a moment's stiffening but it was getting dark. It was sensible to walk hand in hand and he felt her make the decision to relax.

He was allowed to hold her hand. Why did it feel like a momentous decision?

Family. Why were Ewan's last words resonating?

Boris walked at their heels. He'd obviously had a big day and was content to pad along behind them. Even the rabbit that shot out across their path didn't so much as raise his interest.

'He's a good dog,' Rab said into the stillness, mostly because it was something to say. Something to cut through the strange emotions this day had brought.

'He's a great dog.' Mia's hand was still in his and it felt…okay. No, it felt good. 'I was never allowed to have a dog when I was a kid. How about you?'

'Nope.' And then, because the night was very still, because the day had been strange, because her hand was in his, he suddenly found himself talking.

'My dad was…damaged,' he said. 'You've seen the pictures of the twins. Dad's brother died when he was twelve and he was blamed. I can't begin to imagine how that felt, but it cut him off from…well, from a lot. He didn't do relationships. I was a mistake, a fleeting liaison with a woman who didn't believe in abortion but who didn't want me. So I was dumped on Dad.'

'Oh, Rab…'

'Yeah.' He shrugged, and tried to block out the sensations caused by the sudden tightening of her hand. Why was he telling her this? He didn't have a clue, but for some reason he went on.

'Anyway, I was looked after—nannies, child-care, boarding school, the best that money could buy. Some of the nannies were great. One—Luisa—took care of me from the time I was about six to when I was ten. And then she told me her mum was ill back in Switzerland and she had to go home. I felt...well, I felt gutted... but for a farewell gift she brought me a puppy.'

'That's lovely,' Mia said, and by her tone he knew she absolutely approved of the absent Luisa. 'What sort?'

'I'm not sure. A Labrador? A golden retriever? No matter, she was a silly, floppy puppy I called Lulu. Lulu had been my pet name for Luisa and it sort of worked. She had a white-tipped tail. I remember holding her at night and her tail seemed to wriggle, even in sleep.'

'But what happened?' And she knew this story had no happy ending—he knew she knew.

'Boarding school,' he said. 'I'd been a day kid—there are very few schools in Australia which take primary-aged boarders but as soon as Luisa left Dad managed it. So three weeks after Luisa left I was packed off. I remember pleading with Dad to look after Lulu and he promised she'd be taken care of. We had staff, gardeners, a housekeeper, live-in people who could look after her, but when I came home at half-term she was gone.'

'Whoa,' Mia said in a small voice. 'Oh, Rab, that sucks.'

'Yeah,' he said, but then he shrugged. They were in the house grounds now and the lawn was manicured smooth, but still he held her hand. 'But I got over it. Kids do.'

'They do,' she said, sounding stronger now. 'But wow, Rab, you've given me an object lesson.'

'How so?'

'Well,' she said as they neared the front door, 'I thought I had a rough deal as a kid, but the one thing I knew was that Mum loved me. You had what? A nanny and three weeks' worth of puppy? That doesn't come close. So guess what, suddenly I feel lucky. Thank you, Rab.'

They'd reached the veranda. He hauled out the frog key, unlocked the door and stood aside to let her pass. But, instead of going straight in, she paused for a moment and then suddenly raised herself on tiptoe and kissed him. It was fleeting, a moment's touch, and then she backed away.

'Rab, thank you,' she said softly. 'Thank you for tonight, for saving Harry. And thank you too, for marrying me. If I had to choose anyone to save the valley with, I'm very glad it was you.'

'Think nothing of it.' He tried to keep his voice light but it didn't come off. 'We need to wash.'

'So we do,' she agreed. 'Bags the bathroom first.'

'There's a shower in the washhouse outside. I can use that. Take your time.'

'Hooray.'

And he was left in the hall, looking after her.

Boris was still by his side. The big dog gave an anxious whine—this place was strange and his mistress had just departed. Rab found himself kneeling, rubbing the dog behind the ears, trying to impart comfort.

Or taking comfort? He wasn't sure. For some reason Ewan's words were still echoing in his mind.

'It's time you took your family home.'

CHAPTER EIGHT

WIRADJURI HAD BEEN built well before the fashion of en suite or even multiple bathrooms. It therefore had only the one bathroom, but the washhouse—the outside laundry—had been built with an outside shower as well. Which was great. She could do as Rab suggested and take her time getting clean.

And get her thoughts in order.

The bathroom was a picture of Colonial splendour, with a vast freestanding tub, an amazing pedestal sink and a shower big enough for two. She stood under the hot water, letting the sticky mess from blackberries and tree sap wash away, and thought she could even have shared.

As if. The emotions of the day needed time to settle—and she didn't need to get one bit closer to Rab Finlay. The outside washhouse might not be as luxurious but it was much more sensible— and sensible had to be their mantra.

When she finally emerged she almost had

her head together. She donned pyjamas and a well-worn dressing gown—this bride had gone for the modest look in nightwear—and headed to the kitchen, where she found Boris already snoozing under the table, and Rab setting out coffee mugs.

He wasn't looking as modest as she was. He was wearing a clean pair of jeans, but nothing else.

She had a flashback to the sight of him lifting Harry up through the briars—no mean feat, but Rab had pulled him as if he weighed nothing. The sheer strength of the man had astonished her then, and the sight of his body now... Well, it was a body most women would take more than a cursory look at. Gorgeous didn't begin to cut it, and the mass of scratches on his back did nothing to take away the effect of utter... sexiness.

He had his back to her. She stood in the doorway and watched him for a moment, and the realisation suddenly slammed home. *This man is my husband.*

There was still a trickle of fear in the thought, but also...

No! She wasn't going down that road. Not ever.

Sensible, she thought frantically. Sensible!

Thankfully, Ewan's question came back to

her, the elderly doctor's request that she check Rab's cuts and scratches. *'Mia, can you take care of him?'* With a certain amount of effort she let herself think, That's why I'm here. Otherwise she could have gone straight to bed, not come in search of him.

But…would she? Liar, liar, pants on fire, she said under her breath, but then she dived back into the safe thought that they'd been through trauma, and after trauma medics needed to debrief. She *should* have come to find him, even if there weren't scratches all down his back which she needed to treat.

But then he turned, and smiled, and all those logical, reasonable excuses disappeared.

'Tea or coffee?' he asked. The prosaic question should have steadied her but it did no such thing.

'I…yes. Tea. Please.' She paused for a moment and took a long, steadying breath, during which she gave herself a rapid and extremely stern talking-to. Get a grip, woman. 'But I need to clean those scratches'

'That's why I left my shirt off,' he told her. 'I've done my front but I need antiseptic on my back. I could use your help.'

'Let's do it before tea,' she said, thinking the quicker she got this over with the better.

He was already prepared. He had a basin of

hot, soapy water, antiseptic, dressings, tweezers. She winced when she saw the tweezers.

'A couple on my arms had a bit of debris in them,' he explained, and she nodded and attempted to flick an internal switch and become a professional.

'Right. Sit and let me see.'

So he sat, and she stood in her faded dressing gown and checked out every inch of him. Or—thankfully—from his waist up. 'I wear heavy denim for a reason,' he told her.

'Are you sure?' The combination of his shirt and hers hadn't protected him enough.

'I'm sure,' he growled, and she even managed a grin as she moved from scratch to scratch. She was carefully swabbing, making sure nothing was left of the vicious thorns, then applying antiseptic, focusing carefully only on the damage. The growl had been one of defence, and she thought of the many men she'd treated in her career and their reluctance to drop their pants for medical reasons.

'I had a farmer come into Emergency once after a run-in with stinging nettles,' she told him. 'Apparently he was caught short out in the paddocks and didn't notice where he was squatting. His hind quarters were a mess—in the end we gave him antihistamine because it was a severe allergic reaction—but it took us twenty minutes before he let us see. Doc Ewan was away, there was only me and Issy. His reaction was so severe we suspected snake bite, but would he let us look? In the end I had to threaten to bring in the cavalry to hold him down. Marion and Kate from the kitchen. They'd have loved it but he caved before we could call them.'

'You don't need the cavalry for me,' he told her hastily. 'I swear the denim did its job.'

'Lucky you,' she told him and went back to swabbing. 'Ouch. Rab, I'm so sorry you had to do this. Digging your hands through those thorns... You deserve a medal.'

It had been little short of heroic, she thought, shoving his arms down through the thorns.

'There was no choice. All I can say is thanks be that we were there,' he told her. 'And hooray, there's another bonus of our marriage.'

'There are surely bonuses all over the place,' she retorted but her voice must have been strained because he swivelled in his chair and looked up at her.

'Mia, we have done the right thing,' he said gently. 'You call me brave? What you've done is far, far braver. I promise you won't regret it. Ever.'

And what was there in that that made her eyes well? She blinked and blinked again and then applied herself to the very technical detail of putting a plaster on one of the deeper scratches on his arm.

'Not so bad,' he told her, looking down at her handiwork. 'I owe you a new shirt.'

'Yeah, well, we owe you the valley.'

'Maybe we both need to forget that,' he told her. 'Mia, let's call it quits with the gratitude and get on with…a year of being friends?'

She took a deep breath. 'I can live with that.'

'Excellent.' She finished his arm, the last of the wounds, and straightened. He rose. 'Right then, what about you?'

'What about me?'

'You crawled on your stomach out along the branch with no shirt on. That bark was rough and there were briars creeping over. I saw blood before you put the towel back over.'

'You put the towel back over—for which I'm grateful—and I'm fine.' She had been scratched—she'd seen grazes while she'd showered but there was no way…

'You winced then as you stood back. You'll have scratched scar tissue. Mia, I'm not letting you go to bed without checking. Fair's fair.'

'I don't need to be checked, and there's no cavalry here to make me submit,' she said, glowering. The thought of him seeing her scars close-up was intimidating. 'Only Boris, though Boris would hardly protect me.'

'He looks like he would though,' he said thoughtfully, glancing to where Boris was sleeping off his Very Big Day. 'Is that why you got such a big dog? To protect you?'

And there it was again, that flash of fear that was always with her. Harvey in court, yelling as he was led away to start years in prison. 'I'll come for you, you b…'

'Boris is great at cuddling,' she told him, but he was looking at her in an odd way. As if he were trying to figure a puzzle.

'So you got him for cuddles?'

'Yep.' She hesitated. 'Like you should have had with Lulu. I'm very sorry you had to lose her. But I'm fine, Rab. Really. I'll forgo the tea, if you don't mind. I need to go to bed.'

'Mia?'

'Yes.'

'I don't need the cavalry. I'll either check those scratches or I'll pick you up and carry you to the hospital and find someone there who can do it. Choose.'

'Rab…'

'I'm your friend,' he told her gently. 'I've seen your face and I've seen the scars on your side. There's no shock and no shame. Let me see the damage you did tonight.'

'But not my butt or my breasts,' she told him.

'I was wearing jeans and bra all the time. There are no scratches under.'

'Promise?'

'I promise.'

'I'll believe you,' he told her. 'But your back, arms and upper and lower chest. Let's see, Mia.'

'Fine,' she said ungratefully and tugged her pyjama top off, hugged it across her breasts and sat where he'd been sitting. 'Do it.'

Apart from the burns specialist she'd had to visit occasionally for checks on the grafts, no one had seen her chest and side for almost ten years. She was appalled that on this first night of her marriage Rab had seen them, once while they'd swum and now at close range.

The oil had hit her shoulder, splashed up to her face then dripped down over her chest. Her shoulder was a mass of scar tissue. It still had the capacity to make her feel ill when she caught sight of it in the mirror.

But Rab made no comment. He was a surgeon, she told herself. He'd have seen worse, and he was surely treating her now as a doctor. The same way she'd treated him in her role as medic.

Yeah, right. As if she could have cleaned those scratches without that little voice in the back of her head reminding her, *This guy's my husband.*

He wouldn't think anything of it. He had no traumatic marriage in the past, but he must have had lots of girlfriends. She'd known and treated his grandfather and she'd asked about his family. She'd heard the old man's bitterness.

'There's only my grandson and he's a bloody playboy, exactly like his father.'

So Rab had had plenty of women, beautiful women at a guess. He wouldn't be looking at her now as anything but someone he needed to treat.

She sat stock-still while he carefully examined the graze across her chest where she'd dragged herself out along the branch. Rab had done it easily but she'd clung like a limpet and without her shirt her skin—especially the fragile graft skin—had been damaged.

'It's only superficial,' he told her, swabbing with antiseptic. 'But it'll probably weep. I'll put a dressing across the whole graft. It'll protect your sheets if nothing else.'

'Thank you,' she said and sat some more while his skilled surgeon's hands did their thing. And there was no reason why her skin tingled at his touch, why this feeling was suddenly overwhelming her, this sensation that she was… being cared for.

And not medically. What she was feeling was

not remotely similar to how she'd felt as doctors in the past had examined, touched, treated.

'I'm your friend,' he'd said, and it was somehow enveloping her like a warm mist, a fuzzy wrap that made the day's myriad emotions fade to nothing. She needed to think nothing, do nothing, feel nothing... Except that wasn't quite right. Feeling was everything—the soft touch of his fingers, the sensation that he cared.

Her husband.

And that shook her back into reality. She remembered that first night with Harvey. *'I'm your husband.'*

She couldn't stop the shiver and Rab must have felt it. He finished fastening the dressing and stepped back.

'Done. Now tea.'

'I don't think I want...'

'I'm very sure you do,' he told her, and she watched as he made tea, loaded it with sugar, put it in front of her and then watched her as he drank his. It was late at night, they were drinking tea together, he was her husband...

'He wasn't your husband,' Rab said as she set down her mug, and her eyes flew to his. How could he have guessed her thoughts? 'He was a lying piece of filth, and you were never married. What you and I have—this is a contract between adults, between friends, and you're not to think of it as anything else.'

He rose and picked up her mug and set it in the sink, then came around to help her to her feet. Using her good arm, he gently propelled her up, as if he guessed that her world right now seemed weirdly shaky.

'Go to bed, now, Mia,' he told her. 'Today we've saved your valley and we've also saved one trapped kid. That's a great day in anyone's estimation. Well done, Mia, and well done us. Do you think you can sleep?'

'I… Yes.' The sensation of his hand on her arm was doing her head in. He was too big, too bare, too…male.

'Then sleep, Mia,' he told her softly, and before she guessed what he intended he leaned forward and kissed her.

It was as hers had been, once again the lightest of kisses, lips barely brushing her hair, and then he was stepping away from her, smiling with that oh, so amazing smile.

'You've saved the world today, my brave Mia,' he told her. 'What on earth shall we do tomorrow to follow up?'

CHAPTER NINE

How do you know that you're falling in love? Does it take a moment, a sudden flash of certainty? Or does it take a slow dawning, that here might be a woman to cherish for the rest of your life?

Someone he wished to care for—for ever? Was that what love was? Best guess, he supposed it was.

He was sitting on the bank of a meandering creek, among the rocky crags and magnificent bushland that formed the headwaters of the river that burbled its way down to the valley below.

Mia was maybe twenty metres above his head, abseiling down a cliff face. He had no wish to join her and she, having talked him into trying and then watched the grim-faced ascent he'd attempted a couple of months back, had agreed he wasn't meant to be a climber. It hadn't stopped him joining her, though. This Sunday afternoon was now one of many.

The last six months had passed faster than he'd thought possible. He'd imagined he'd leave his high-powered city medicine, help a bit at the hospital, keep up the pretence of being a married couple, maybe do a spot of study and put his life on hold for a year. Instead, he surely hadn't put his life on hold. For now at least, this was life itself.

Part of that life was Mia, and she certainly hadn't put her life on hold either. She hadn't kept still for a moment.

'If I have free board for a year I might as well make myself useful,' she'd decreed within days of moving into Wiradjuri.

The gardens had been maintained by Nora, but the house itself had suffered decades of neglect. That first morning, after the drama of the blackberries, he'd woken late to find her deep in soot, intent on cleaning out the ancient fire stove.

'It's fantastic,' she'd told him and pointed in disgust at the grimy two-ring burner his grandfather had obviously used. 'He used that when he had an Aga! Wow, Rab, wait till I get it working, these things are awesome.'

'So you're intending to spend the first day of your honeymoon cleaning my stove,' he'd said faintly, and she'd grinned. There'd been a smudge of soot on her nose. She was filthy. She must still be hurting from the grazes she'd suffered the night before, but she'd looked...happy.

'Yep,' she'd told him. 'At the end of the year I'll be leaving you with a legacy. No matter what you do with this place, it'll look fantastic. And I'll love doing it, Rab,' she'd told him, seeing his look of doubt. 'I can't bear standing still.'

She couldn't. She'd thrown herself headlong into the restoration of the old house, and he'd been slowly caught up in her enthusiasm. He found himself painting with her, scrubbing, hauling up old carpets and sanding ancient floorboards. Enjoying himself.

The medicine too... The little hospital was magnificently run but it had taken him only days to realise how much more service it could provide with two doctors instead of one. Mia hadn't been backward in drawing him into that. He'd imagined his surgery skills would be put on the backburner for a year, but she'd had none of it.

'Ewan has anaesthetist skills,' she'd told him. 'The locals hate leaving the valley for health care, so why not do the smaller stuff here?'

He did, and there was enough demand to keep his skills up. As well, he found himself enjoying the normal demands of family medicine. He enjoyed even more the house calls Ewan had tentatively asked him to share, driving across the valley to treat people at home.

He'd never thought of it—the huge advantage of patients being able to stay in their own homes while they either recovered from accidents or illnesses, or faded towards end of life. It hadn't taken him long to realise what a gift it was.

The first few times Mia had accompanied him. 'You know Doc Finlay? He's one of us now. I've come with him just to make sure he doesn't muck up. He's a city doctor, you know, and who can tell what weird new-fangled treatments he might try out on you.'

Mia's infectious cheer, her laughter, her care, had made such visits relaxed and fun. It had taken few such house calls to realise how much she was loved, and when she'd decreed he'd graduated into doing them on his own he'd felt more than a stab of loss.

But then there'd been the weekends. If it rained they stayed at Wiradjuri and worked inside, but if the day was fine Mia would be tossing her climbing gear into the back of her little Mini and heading for the hills.

For the first few weeks he'd assumed she'd want space and he'd watched her go in silence, thinking she probably needed time without him, but every time she'd come back exhausted but with a glow of peace and satisfaction. It had him intrigued.

'It's awesome out there,' she'd said one Saturday evening as she tucked into the casserole he'd prepared—the initial plan had been to eat separately but that had pretty much dissolved the first time she'd tasted his cooking. 'You should come.'

'How on earth did you get into rock climbing?'

'I did all sorts of stuff to get my strength back,' she told him. 'Rehab started it, and then the need to fend for myself. I learned karate first.' She grinned. 'So maybe I should warn you—don't mess with me. I'm a fourth dan karate black belt. You don't know what that means? Just hope you never get to find out.' She chuckled. Maybe the look on his face warranted it—he surely hadn't been able to hide his incredulity. 'And then I got distracted by other things,' she'd told him. 'Climbing's awesome.'

He'd felt…stunned. 'Karate. Rock climbing.' He'd had to know more. 'Would you mind if I join you?'

'Of course not. Why should I?'

So the next day they'd headed out together. Boris was thus relegated to the back seat of the Mini. He was almost glowering with displeasure—it was a tight squeeze—but at least he was happy to be with his two favourite people.

'He's falling for you,' Mia had said comfortably. 'Mind, I've seen you feeding him toast. Give Boris toast and he's anybody's.'

Then she'd introduced him to her world. She climbed like she'd been born to it, but he'd tried and fast decided he was all for keeping his feet safely on the ground.

It didn't worry her. She was an independent woman, he thought, watching her now as she abseiled down the cliff she'd just spider-climbed her way up. She didn't need him watching over her. But at some point in the past few months he'd begun to realise that he wouldn't mind if she did.

They'd been six months married. She talked of the end of their marriage with nonchalance.

'I'm going to miss Wiradjuri when I go back to my place,' she'd said a few weeks ago. She'd hauled a great dust-covered chandelier—a chandelier, for heaven's sake!—down from the ceiling of the drawing room and was lovingly polishing each crystal. 'This is awesome,' she'd said. 'I'm sure you can buy them in plastic, but if I hung something like this in my little cottage I'd have to duck every time I made myself a cup of tea.'

But there'd been no regret in her voice. No envy. Just a statement of fact.

Which was what she was all about, he thought as he watched her. She hardly seemed to look forward or look back. She was smart, loyal and kind. She was also funny, but it seemed to him that she carried her gentle humour almost as armour.

And she still needed that armour, he thought. He saw the ache in her arms at the end of a day's climbing, how she hugged herself when she thought he couldn't see. He thought of what she was doing now, climbing, stretching that inelastic scar tissue to the limit. He thought of the emotional scars inside, and the more he knew her, the more he wanted to protect her...hold her.

But she didn't want to be held. He knew that. That first night, when he'd kissed her, that faint brush of lips on her hair, he'd seen her reaction. She'd kissed him but that had been on her terms. When he'd kissed her...

She didn't want it. This year was working only because they were acting as friends, nothing more.

He was starting to want...more.

'Hey!' She was on the ground again, struggling to rid herself of her harness and bouncing happily back to where he'd set up their picnic rug. 'That was fabulous. You should see the view from the top. You two lazybones are missing out on so much.' She plonked herself down, dived into the picnic basket and retrieved a sandwich. 'Yum.'

'Boris and I walked right up to the top of the falls,' he said, with dignity. 'We probably ended up higher than you, and we didn't risk calling the Angels of Mercy once.'

'You mean you're doing a public service by not risking calling the emergency services?' Her voice was muffled by sandwich.

'Exactly.'

'You're a pair of wusses,' she told him and grinned and then turned back to look out over the valley. 'This is the best. My happy place.'

And there was that thought again... Was he falling in love?

He'd thought he was in love before. He and Annabel had been part of the same set at university—they'd been friends. They'd had fun together, started their medical lives together, worked hard, played hard and finally moved in together. But almost as soon as they had, things had started to seem...distant. He remembered a creeping sense of claustrophobia he couldn't shake.

He remembered that last night. He'd come home late after an appalling shift at the hospital. A car crash. Three children dead, one under his hands on the operating table. He'd been sick with the horror.

Annabel had found him at three in the morning, sitting on the balcony, drinking whisky, staring at nothing.

'Why didn't you wake me?' she'd asked.

'We don't both need to be upset.'

She'd tried to take him into her arms, but he couldn't let his body melt into hers. The horror was too real. The only way he could deal with it was to hold himself tight, internalise the pain, scrunch it into a tight ball and tuck it where it couldn't be seen.

The next day he'd walked and walked, and when he'd finally returned to their apartment something seemed to have died within them both.

Annabel was still his friend, but she was happily married now, to another friend, Max. He'd attended their wedding and Max had come up to him afterwards, enveloped him in a man hug and thanked him—for not marrying her. 'She says you guys broke up because you didn't need her. You must have had rocks in your head, mate, but I'm grateful. I need this woman so much—I'm just so lucky she needs me right back.'

There'd been tears in Max's eyes as he'd

gazed at his bride, but Rab hadn't understood how anyone could show emotion like that. He still didn't.

Love?

But now he was watching a woman, grubby with exertion, eating a mammoth ham and pickle sandwich while she absentmindedly rubbed her bad shoulder with her free hand. His heart was twisting with feelings he was struggling to deal with. He'd never expected this, never wanted it, but now...

Mia made it quite clear that she valued her independence above all else. He'd held that as inviolable, but watching her enjoy her sandwich, watching her turn her face to soak in the glint of sunlight through the trees, he was feeling things and he didn't have a clue how to deal with them.

He was thinking of Max's long-ago emotion. And he was starting to feel...the same?

No. Max had talked as if he needed Annabel. Could Mia need him?

Her hand was still rubbing her shoulder absentmindedly, as if this was a long-term ache, something she barely thought about. Which was exactly what it was, he thought. Her scars, physical and emotional, were just a part of her.

'Let me do it,' he said, and moved to her side, removing her hand and letting his fingers massage what he knew was the scar tissue under her windcheater. He couldn't see it—after that first night when she'd reluctantly agreed to let him clean her grazes she'd stayed firmly covered. Now he felt her whole body stiffen.

'Hey, I'm a crap climber,' he told her. 'But I once did a massage course. Actually, a girl-friend and I both did one. We thought it might improve our relationship.'

'And did it?' She was still stiff.

'Nope,' he said cheerfully. 'Annabel thought the masseur was the sexiest guy she'd ever met. Obviously her heart wasn't in it.'

'Obviously.' She thought about it for a bit. 'So if you'd been a bit sexier you might be married to someone called Annabel.'

'I guess.' Who knew?

She turned and gave him a thoughtful look, seemingly assessing all of him.

'Yeah,' she said and grinned. 'I get that.'

'You don't think I'm sexy?'

'Hey, I'm not allowed to think you're sexy. This is a marriage of convenience.'

'But if it wasn't?'

'How can I tell? I haven't even seen you in pyjamas yet.'

'You've seen me in less than my PJs.'

'Not the same,' she said, definitely.

'You can tell a man's sexy by the pyjamas he wears?'

'Certainly you can,' she told him. 'Let me tell you, very few men can carry PJs off, and I'm speaking from the position of someone who's checked out thousands. The number of pyjamas-clad guys I've seen in my lifetime…'

He thought of his pyjamas. He usually slept without anything, but he did own one set. Boxers and T-shirt. There'd been a Kris Kringle at the hospital last year and his senior anaesthetist, a woman in her sixties, had drawn his number. He'd opened her gift at the theatre staff's Christmas party and the T-shirt's logo had been received with howls of mirth: *Keep talking. I'm diagnosing you.*

It had been a crack at his distancing. The theatre staff—almost a family they spent so much time together—gave him a hard time. 'We find the juiciest gossip and all you do is listen. We know you listen to everyone. How about sharing?'

That was pretty much the same accusation Annabel had thrown at him, but now… He was looking at Mia in the sunlight, he was feeling the tension in her shoulders and he thought maybe it wouldn't hurt to try and lessen the distance.

'Mia, what would you say if I asked you out on a date?' he asked, tentatively because it seemed like an infringement on the rules they'd carefully set themselves. He didn't want to mess with that. He couldn't.

'A date.' His hands were still on her shoulders, but he felt her stiffen again.

'Yep.' There was a moment's silence and then he added, 'It's what happens when a boy meets a girl and he wants to get to know her better.'

'You don't think living in the same house for six months could do the same thing?'

'I think living in the same house for six months has made me realise I'd like to get to know you better.'

'I don't want…' She'd practically frozen. He had the sense to remove his hands and back away a little.

'You don't want to get to know me better?'

'Rab, I can't.'

'Because?'

'I don't need anyone.'

He thought she did but he wasn't going there. 'I don't need anyone either,' he told her. 'But it doesn't stop me thinking…what we have…it could be good.'

'Or it could be a disaster.'

'Would one date, where we let ourselves be… open to possibilities…necessarily risk disaster? It'd be like web dating. We come with a list of prepared questions and see if there's the faintest possibility we might be compatible.'

'I already know you're afraid of heights. How compatible's that?'

'And you're grumpy before your first coffee in the morning,' he retorted. 'But there'll be other questions, I'm sure.'

'You're thinking of the compatibility of sharing the one toothpaste tube?'

'No!' he said with haste, and she chuckled.

'There you go then. Totally incompatible. Do you know how much waste there is in toothpaste tubes? The one advantage of sharing would be buying those huge ones, but the squeezing has to be done at the bottom.'

'Obviously incompatible,' he agreed, and his gaze caught hers and held. In challenge? 'But we could put it on our list to discuss. One date, Mia. If our lists coincide, then maybe another date in a fortnight or so? Another list. There's no rush, Mia, but maybe…' He hesitated but decided there was no point in not saying it. 'Mia, we have six months. The way I'm feeling…'

'You shouldn't be feeling.' She sounded all at once terrified. 'I told you. This is a business arrangement. No emotions.'

'There aren't any emotions,' he told her. 'And there won't be in the future if that's what you want, but now we're at the six-month mark…would it be possible to have dinner, check our lists and recalibrate?' And then he smiled, holding her gaze, trying to win a smile in return. 'There's actually a magnificent restaurant in Colambool. Rhonda was telling me she and Gary went there a few weeks back to celebrate their wedding anniversary. She says you'd love it.'

'Have you been talking about me to Rhonda?'

'Hey, not guilty.' Discussing Mia—discussing anyone but patients—well, that pyjama top held some truth. 'But she talks to me about you. She said she's never seen you go out on a date in the almost ten years she's known you, and if I wanted a place to celebrate our six-month anniversary…'

'Oh, for heaven's sake…'

'So how about it?' he asked and discovered he was holding his breath.

She stared at him. He could still see a trace of panic in her gaze but there was something else. An internal war?

She'd had such trauma. How tempting would it be to step, just for a moment, into a place where she could do something she'd never done—go to a fancy restaurant on a date? How simple was that?

But, almost unconsciously, her hand went to her

face, to her scarring. No to that, he thought savagely, and he put his own hand up to cover hers.

'Mia,' he said gently, 'you're beautiful. You're a brave, fun woman who climbs cliffs that take my breath away. You should know that you're stunning. How about accepting that about yourself, at least, just for one night, and come out and just have fun? Do you have the courage to do that?'

Their hands stayed where they were, hers on her face, his covering hers. Their gazes stayed locked.

Please.

It was an internal plea and it reverberated over and over in his head. For some reason this seemed one of the most important moments in his life.

Please...

And finally, finally she closed her eyes. She lifted her hand from her cheek and pushed his hand away at the same time, and then she opened her eyes and gave a firm businesslike nod.

'I guess you did try and climb the cliffs with me,' she managed. 'I suppose I can at least try your fancy restaurant.'

He grinned, aware of a surge of pleasure totally out of proportion to the concept of one woman accepting one date.

'And your list?'

'My list's easy,' she told him. 'Independence.'

'Let's start with toothpaste and work up,' he suggested. 'Who knows, Mia? Anything's possible.'

CHAPTER TEN

WHAT TO WEAR on a date?

Why to think about even going on a date?

Whoa.

She should have pulled out. It was a dumb thing to do, breaking every rule she'd made for herself regarding relationships. Never look at a man that way. Never think about being anything other than totally independent.

On Monday she'd woken resolved to tell him to forget the idea. Unfortunately there'd been an early morning call and Rab had left in a hurry. An appendectomy. Then she'd arrived at work herself, to a frantic call from the principal of the local school. Three kids had arrived with a rash and the principal was panicking. Measles?

Measles was unlikely—as far as Mia knew, almost every kid in the valley was vaccinated— but with Rab and Ewan both caught up with the appendectomy she'd headed to the school herself.

It took time to get the story out of kids who'd been told not to deviate as they'd walked to school, but it finally emerged. It seemed the kids had detoured to roll down grassy slopes in a nearby freshly mown paddock. This looked like some sort of allergic reaction to one of the grasses. As soon as she had the truth she administered antihistamine. The rashes had started fading almost straight away, but it had taken more time to reassure the principal and three lots of worried parents.

By the time she'd got back to the hospital Rab had already made the booking at the restaurant—and worse! Rhonda's sister-in-law was, apparently, a chef there and had taken Rab's call. And had immediately rung Rhonda. 'Hey, guess who we have coming?'

Mia was a loved figure in the valley. As a whole, the valley's population was intrigued and delighted with this marriage of convenience—not only had it saved the valley but it had also brought them another doctor. Now, with the valley realising there was only six months left before Dr Finlay was due to leave again, pretty much every staff member was egging them on to make the arrangement permanent. The news of the restaurant booking had thus spread all over the hospital by lunch time.

By the end of that Monday almost every female member of staff had put in their opinion of what she should wear, and by the time she finally saw Rab she'd realised he was getting the same treatment. He'd even been looking a bit...hunted.

Which had sort of made her laugh. Which had sort of made it impossible to disappoint everyone by saying she was pulling out.

So here she was, the night of the...date, staring into the mirror at a Mia she didn't recognise.

At Maira?

Her old name was suddenly echoing in her head, almost with longing. It was the name she'd discarded along with her identity when she'd moved here. Harvey was a control freak, a possessive, violent bully. She'd received a few messages in those early days, notes appearing from prison, via sources the police couldn't trace. He blamed her for his prison sentence and he still thought he owned her. 'I bought you for your father's debt,' he'd told her. 'And I'll come for you. No matter where you are, no matter how long it takes, you're mine.'

'We'll protect you as much as we can,' the authorities had told her when she'd shown them. 'It's nine years till he's due for parole though. Hopefully he'll have moved on.'

She knew Harvey, though, and she knew he

wouldn't move on. She needed to protect herself. A name-change?

So she'd become Mia, a quiet, hard-working nurse in remote New South Wales. Mia, not related to Maira.

Mia, who was standing in front of the mirror now, looking at herself in a dress Rhonda had found when she'd browbeaten her into taking a shopping trip to Colambool.

'Something smart but plain,' Mia had decreed, and Rhonda and the shop assistant had raised their eyebrows and proceeded to ignore her. 'I reckon this'd suit you,' Rhonda had said.

The dress was crimson, elegant—and maybe it was a little bit plain, except what it did for her wasn't plain. Mia had slipped it on and almost gasped.

It had a hint of the oriental, a mandarin collar, with a slit down her throat so she could just see a hint of the swell of her breasts. It had three-quarter sleeves with a line of tiny slits all the way down. She could see a hint of bare arm but not enough to reveal the scarring underneath.

And the rest of the dress—yes, it was plain, but it was *her* dress. It fitted her as if it had been stitched onto her, every curve delineated, clinging close to her knees, with a final slit on the side allowing a glimpse of thigh as she moved.

She'd stared at it in the shop and she'd felt... panicked. But also something else.

A longing to be Maira again?

Or someone else entirely?

Rhonda had also towed her to the hairdresser. 'Let's just see if there's a way you can wear it that's a bit sexier than a braid.'

She'd lost thirty centimetres of her hair, removing enough weight to allow her to play with it. The stylist had shown her how to twist it into a loose knot but tease a few curls down, their twisting enough to distract from the scarring on her face. They were still there, the scars, but as she looked at herself in the mirror now she thought, *This is what I could have been. I could have been Maira.*

Enough introspection. She took a deep breath, slipped on the shoes Rhonda had decreed she bought as well—glossy black stilettos, for heaven's sake!—and she walked back out to the living room.

To Rab.

He turned to face her—and froze.

The sight of him was enough to freeze her as well, she thought. He was wearing the suit he'd worn for the wedding. He looked stunning, absurdly handsome, the kind of man any woman would be proud to be seen with.

And the thought was suddenly front and centre. *He was her husband.*

'Mia!' He said her name almost as a sigh. He didn't have to compliment, didn't have to say she looked beautiful. His expression said it all.

And just for a moment she forgot the scars. She was Maira again, a kid leafing through those magazines her mother had brought home, looking at lives she could never have but allowed to dream. Maybe she could dream again. Just for tonight, she told herself. One night…

'Hey, we scrub up okay,' she managed, trying to break the moment—because it had to be broken. Even if he was looking at her…like that… it was just a dream.

'We do indeed,' he said, and he sounded as if he was feeling pretty much the same. 'Mia, you're always beautiful, but tonight…'

'Dress-ups,' she said, almost roughly. 'I'll be back in scrubs on Monday. This is one night only.'

'Then let's make the most of it,' he told her. 'My car, Mia, because I refuse to take you looking like this in a car that smells like dog.'

'There's an insult,' she said and grinned down at Boris, who was sniffing her legs with faint interest. Her legs obviously smelled…different.

Of course they did, she thought. Everything she wore was different. For this night, everything about her seemed different.

'I've bought you a great bone to make up for our desertion,' she told Boris, speaking a bit too fast, diving for the refrigerator, forcing herself to be prosaic. 'Okay. Let's give the dog a bone and we can go.'

She'd never been on a 'date', and if this was to be the first then hopefully it would be a good one.

Mia's life was divided into two sections, Harvey and post Harvey. Even post Harvey he'd controlled her actions. She was determined to stay independent for the rest of her life. What she was doing tonight was risky, an aberration, but now she'd agreed to it there was no reason why she shouldn't enjoy it, was there?

If there was, it certainly wasn't caused by the restaurant. Mountain Hollow was one of those places written up in trendy magazines as a destination in itself, a foody paradise as well as a location to die for. It was settled in a hollow in the mountains behind Colambool. Built on a platform overlooking the same river that ran down to Cockatoo Valley, it was almost completely disguised by thick bushland. Cars were parked at the top of the slope and a gorgeous path, lit by demure side lights, led the way downward.

The restaurant itself looked welcoming but plain. It was only when you walked inside that you saw the view below, the tumbling waters of the falls, the boulder-strewn river, the whole lit by lights that seemed so natural they looked almost like stars drifting down from the night sky.

She and Rab were ushered to a table right by the window, where the tree tops were so close she felt she could almost touch them. Rab held the chair for her. She sat, feeling like she'd stepped into another world, as outside the window a couple of tiny sugar gliders hung on a branch and peered in.

'They're admiring your dress,' Rab said, and she looked quickly at him and found he was smiling. He must be used to this sort of place, she told herself.

'It's stunning,' he said, and she knew then that he wasn't used to it. That this was taking his breath away too.

'How did you find out about it?' she breathed.

'Rhonda. Remember?'

'Of course.' And the fact that Rhonda's sister-in-law was a chef here—that'd explain why they had what was obviously the best table in the house.

Weirdly, that knowledge made her feel better. That it wasn't completely down to Rab. He wasn't pulling the strings.

Was he?

'I feel a bit like Cinderella,' she confessed. 'Any minute now you'll look across the table and find I've turned into a pumpkin.'

He smiled but shook his head. 'No chance. Not here. Rhonda assured me there's a choice on the menu, and I can't abide pumpkin. One of my nannies thought pumpkin soup was easy to make and good for me. Pumpkin is definitely banned from this table.'

The look on his face made her chuckle, and suddenly it was okay. Not so much a date then, she told herself. Just a special night out with a guy who'd become...a friend.

And then the waiter bore down on them with a menu to make her gasp—there was no pumpkin in sight! Champagne was poured and she decided to forget about Cinderella-like transitions. She was twenty-nine and she'd never been in a place like this before. Rab was a friend, a gorgeous, handsome male, but still just a friend for all that. And there were decisions to be made. Lobster patties as entrée? Why not?

She glanced again at Rab and he was smiling. Just at her.

And—just for this night—she tilted her chin

and smiled back, a wide, all-encompassing smile that seemed to almost break something inside her. Leaving her...open?

No. Nothing was changing, this was just a fabulous night.

Cinderella? Bring it on, she told herself. Pumpkins could wait.

She was gorgeous. What was more, she seemed to have decided to make the most of every minute of this night.

She was eating as if she were in a dream, savouring each mouthful, and as he watched her, weirdly, he also found himself thinking of Cinderella. She looked as if she were drifting in a fairy tale from which she expected to emerge, if not at midnight then some time in the future. Soon?

And his own thoughts crystallised. The more he watched her, the more he wanted to make that fairy tale real. To make her safe, happy, secure. To care for her, to cherish her, to look after her for ever. Surely she deserved it.

This feeling had been growing on him for months and tonight, watching her glow with happiness, watching her shrug off the air of defensiveness that she almost always had, he knew for certain.

He wanted her for always.

He couldn't say it now, though. It'd be rushing her, to take this first night when she'd lowered her defences and try to push it further. So he ate and drank and talked and laughed and the night seemed to melt into a pool of perfection. And when coffee was served, along with tiny strawberry and chocolate meringues, barely a taste but just enough to end the perfect dinner, he thought he didn't want this night to end. Ever.

'Walk down to the river with me,' he suggested, and she looked startled.

'Can we?'

'We can.' He'd checked this place out on the website. The pathway they'd used from the car park meandered on, still lit, so they could walk right down to the floodlit waterfall.

There was a moment's hesitation—and then came that smile again, the relaxed smile that seemed so rare it was a jewel itself.

'Why not?' she whispered, and it was as if she were talking to herself. And he knew she was, and he also knew that he was blessed.

'I'm wearing high heels, in case you hadn't noticed.'

'I had noticed.' Wow, had he noticed. 'But I'm here to help you.'

He rose and held out his hand. That brought another moment's hesitation, and he could almost hear the words echoing in her head.

Why not?
Let's put the risk aside.

They walked silently down the path leading to the falls. Still hand in hand, because the path wasn't exactly flat and her heels *were* high, so surely holding his hand was…sensible?

There was near silence, apart from the sound of water tumbling into the pool below the falls, then splashes as the flow rippled along the rock-strewn stream beside the path. Then there were the whispers of night creatures, possums, sugar gliders, rock wallabies, creatures who could see them but were safe in the undergrowth. Once a tiny echidna waddled across the path in front of them, and behind came its harassed mum, obviously fretting about these human intruders in her domain.

The sight made Mia smile. The night made her smile. The feel of Rab's hand holding hers made her feel…cherished?

Cherished. What would it be like to be cherished by such a man? To let go of her rigid control. To let her hand lie where it was…for ever.

No. The night was a dream. This whole scene was a dream, part of a fantasy that surely had to shatter, but not yet. Please not yet.

And then they reached the foot of the falls. The clever lights were shimmering from above, not so bright that they disturbed the night but enough to shimmer and twinkle on the foam of falling water.

They stood silently, watching, taking in its beauty. Almost unconsciously, Rab's arm came around her and she let herself sink against him. His warmth. His strength.

It was fine. No, it was better than fine, and she had no need to worry. For now, this was indeed a fairy tale. She'd wake at midnight—or even tomorrow, she thought dreamily, if she let this fairy tale continue. But for tonight…

His arm tightened and he twisted her so he was gazing down at her.

'Mia,' he said softly, 'I really want to kiss you.'

'I guess that's good,' she whispered back. 'Because I surely want to kiss you.'

He smiled but he didn't kiss her straight away. He turned her within his hold, then cupped her face with his hands. She tilted her chin, aching for contact, but instead he searched her face.

'Mia,' he said softly, 'I'll never hurt you, I swear.'

And then, finally, gloriously, magically, he lowered his head—and he kissed her.

What had he expected?

Rab had kissed women before—many women. His grandfather's obvious labelling of him as a playboy wasn't exactly unfounded, and the feel of a woman's mouth on his wasn't new.

Except this was Mia, and this most definitely was new.

For the moment she tilted her chin, raising her mouth to his, waiting to be kissed, he was hit by a realisation so powerful that it shook something inside him that seemed almost…primeval.

This woman trusts me.

This woman is giving herself to me.

Of course it was no such thing. This was only a kiss, a moment at the end of a glorious night. This was no promise of a future.

Yet the moment his mouth met hers, from the moment when her arms came almost instinctively around his chest, from the moment he tasted her, held her, felt her warmth, her wonder, her…trust?…the night seemed almost to dissolve.

That such a woman could let him kiss her… That he could hold her…

He felt as if the most precious thing in the world, the most fragile jewel, was surrendering herself to him. He kissed her, he held her, and the night seemed to dissolve in a mist of heat and desire.

But more than that. For Rab it seemed almost as if they were merging, as if part of her was becoming…his. He'd hold her safe, he thought. He'd give as much as he could, he'd give and give. Nothing could hurt her again. He swore it almost unconsciously as the kiss went on.

He loved her.

Now all he had to do was convince her that this was not for one night.

This was for ever.

And when finally the cool of the night closed in and it was time to meander back along the path, climb into his gorgeous car and make the trip back to Wiradjuri, the sense of wonder seemed to stay with them. Boris roused himself from his bed beside the kitchen stove and greeted them, but it was time for Rab to head to his end of the house and Mia the other.

But of course they paused and suddenly Rab was kissing her again—or was it the other way around? Then he was holding her at arm's length, his eyes questioning.

'Mia?'

And she knew what he was asking and the answer came, strong and true.

'Yes.'

'Are you sure? Mia, I won't take advantage...'

'You can take all the advantage you like,' she whispered. 'Because yes, I'm very, very sure.'

Except...was she?

CHAPTER ELEVEN

SHE WOKE, CRADLED in his arms, her bare skin against his. Her body felt sated with warmth and sleep and love.

She felt as if she were…home.

All those resolutions, she thought. All that swearing that never again would she be dependent on a man. On anyone. Had it come to nothing?'

Did it really matter if she trusted him? This man was so far from Harvey it was as if they were different species.

At some time during the night Rab had whispered that he loved her. She might even have said the same. Who knew what she'd said? It was all a dream, one she never wanted to wake from.

He'd made love to her. *Love.* It was a strange word.

Once upon a time she'd had romantic dreams of what love could be. She'd even thought the act of making love could be beautiful. That, however, had been an idea gleaned from reading romance novels, the romantic ideal.

Harvey had knocked that out of her, using her body at will, and for years she'd thought she'd never want sex again. But when Rab had touched her his had been a touch that had said the control was still hers. It had been a featherlike kiss as he'd helped her slip off her clothes, a caress of fingers on her cheek, his eyes questioning, as if he knew she was fearful. As if a gesture from her would have made him pull back.

You're in charge, his body language had said, and it had made her feel...powerful. As if she really could pull back. As if this night was all about her pleasure, if she wished it.

Did he understand domestic abuse? Had that been part of his medical training? How had he known what a huge step it had been, to trust?

Whatever, however, suddenly she'd felt as if she could do this. No, she would! She wanted it. Her body had been alight with sensations she'd never felt before. When he'd been naked before her, she'd felt as if she'd never seen a man naked before. Her whole body had blazed with heat and desire, and when they'd fallen onto the sheets she'd taken him and taken him and taken him—and in the end the fierceness of her love-making had almost frightened her.

At some time in the night Rab had pulled back, just a little, so she could see the gleam of his smile in the moonlight filtering through the window.

'Hey,' he'd said, laughing, but with a huskiness that told her his passion matched her own, 'we can sleep a little too, love, if we need. We have all the time in the world.'

But did they? That was a concept that almost had her retreating into that bad place in her head. But then he'd kissed the hollow of her throat, and her body had arched all of its own accord. The future—and the past—were forgotten. And when they'd finally slept she'd thought she was…happy.

And now she lay, sated, warm, deeply content, and Rab's words were replaying in her head. Maybe there could be a future.

And then there was a sharp rap on the front door. She heard Boris bark. Rab stirred, still holding her close.

'What the…?' Rab muttered. When a medical call came she knew they'd be wide awake in seconds, but at this time on a Sunday morning, when Ewan was on call and their phones were working… Surely this wasn't medical. She heard Rab's confusion and knew it matched her own. 'What time is it?

She twisted slightly in his arms so she could see the bedside clock. *His* bedside clock. She'd slept the night in his bed and right now she wanted to stay here for ever.

'Just past nine,' she murmured and felt his arms tighten.

'Just past nine on a Sunday,' he said, kissing her bare shoulder. Her scarred shoulder.

It didn't make one scrap of difference. Right now she felt beautiful. Right now she didn't feel scarred at all.

'I think we didn't get enough sleep,' she murmured, and he chuckled and rolled over to kiss her more deeply.

'We had better things to do,' he said, and his kiss was languorous, long, wonderful.

But then the knock came again and Boris's barking reached a crescendo.

'Someone might be stuck in our blackberries again,' she managed, and then heard what she'd said.

Our blackberries. Joint possession?

Where was her heart taking her?

'Catastrophe? It has to be an earthquake at least to warrant this,' he said and sighed and sat up and pulled on his trousers.

She headed for her room and found a dressing gown, then made her way through to where Rab was opening the front door.

There were two men and a woman on the doorstep. One of the men and the woman were wearing suits, corporate style, a style you didn't see in Cockatoo Valley all that much. The woman had what looked like some sort of camera, a tiny thing attached to her jacket. The younger man was wearing jeans and a shiny leather jacket, with slicked back hair, designer sunglasses, cool trainers. Together they seemed an entirely intimidating presence, and Mia found herself instinctively taking a step back, wishing she had something on under her dressing gown. Wishing she could hide her face.

'Good morning.' The older man spoke first, sounding brisk and efficient. 'We're sorry to disturb you, but we've been asked by Mr Finlay here to do a spot check.'

'Mr Finlay?' Rab said, blankly. He was standing in the doorway, in trousers but nothing else, as confused as Mia.

'This is Mr Noel Finlay. I believe he's a relation of yours,' the older man said calmly, 'from England. I'm George Howard and this is Miss Maria Stein. We're from Howard Stein Legal, based in Sydney. Mr Finlay and two of his cousins have contacted us, asking us to find out if your marriage is all that you say it is.'

'I'm sorry...' Rab sounded stunned but the legal monotone continued.

'Mr Finlay's been informed that you are indeed married,' the man said. 'But he and his siblings believe it's a marriage made to fulfil the requirements of the will, not a true marriage. We've done some research and have found the marriage was only proposed after a meeting here six weeks before your birthday. The accusation is that you hadn't met beforehand, and that this has been organised only to rob our clients of their rightful inheritance. In short, to defraud. We've done our groundwork. This visit is the culmination of that research, and we now need to warn you that this conversation is being recorded and videoed via my colleague's video camera.'

'Is that legal?' Rab asked mildly, and to Mia's astonishment he sounded, if anything, slightly amused. 'Body cameras? Aren't they used for crime scenes?'

'If you're defrauding our client from what's rightfully his, then it is a crime scene.'

'You don't have our permission to film, or to record. And we're within our legal rights to kick you off the property,' Rab said, still mildly. 'You're trespassing.'

'What's wrong with her?'

It was the young guy speaking now, stepping

forward, jaw jutted belligerently. He was staring at Mia, who'd tried to retreat to the shadows. She'd tugged her dressing gown around her, but she was acutely aware that it was thin and there was nothing underneath. At some time in the night Rab had unfastened her hair, and unruly curls tangled every which way. She wore none of the light concealer she usually used to conceal the starkness of her scars.

She felt exposed, scarred, completely off balance.

But then Rab turned and smiled at her. It was a quick smile, meant only for her—a message? Courage, that smile said. Let's play these people at their own game.

How could one smile say that? She didn't know, but as Rab reached for her hand and drew her forward she found herself responding with...trust.

Why was that her first reaction? Why was it so deeply, deeply important?

'Are you talking about my wife?' He had her now, his arm around her, turning so they both faced outward. 'There's nothing wrong with Mia.' And his gaze met the young man's and held. There was something in his expression, something implacable, something hard, and Mia wasn't surprised to see the young man take a step back.

But the belligerence was still there. 'I told you,' the young guy muttered to the lawyers. 'I forgot. The people we talked to told us about the scars. Look at her. He's rich already, a city surgeon, he has everything he wants and then he decides to come here and marry *her*.' And he said *her* in such a way that even the lawyers flinched. 'Why would he do that if he didn't want the money?'

'Mr Finlay...' the male lawyer said in a warning voice but the young man wouldn't be stopped.

'It's a con. For him to marry her...'

'Enough.' Rab's controlled amusement had ceased. 'Get off my land,' he said, and there was something in his voice that made everyone there flinch. Recalibrate. Figure Rab was not to be messed with.

The lawyers certainly got it.

'Mr Finlay, stop,' the lawyer said quickly, harshly, and he was watching Rab's face. He knew they'd gone too far—and this was being recorded. 'Dr and Mrs Finlay, on behalf of our client I apologise for those very personal remarks. Could you forget them, please? Mr Finlay, please go back to the car and remain there. I believe we can ask the questions we need to without your presence.'

'But...'

'Go,' the lawyer said, still watching Rab's face. 'Or he *will* get us thrown off for trespass. He's entitled. Leave this to us.'

'Go, Noel,' the woman said. 'We'll handle this.'

There was a loaded silence and then the young man gave an angry huff and turned and stalked back to the car. 'They've obviously just woken up,' he threw over his shoulder. 'Make 'em show you where they've been sleeping. It's a con, I tell you. A bloody con.'

He climbed into the car and slammed the door, and they were left with two lawyers standing on the doorstep, looking apologetic. But also…determined.

'Dr Finlay, we apologise once again for our client's comments,' the male lawyer said, and Mia was aware the female had stepped back a little. So her camera could get a better view? 'But he's jet lagged, and he and his family have put considerable effort into making this happen.'

'A scheduled interview would have been in order,' Rab growled. He'd tugged Mia close against him, making it seem as if they were one. A couple, woken from sleep, bewildered by this intrusion. As they were.

There was no need for Mia to shake. Why was she? It must have been Noel's voice, she thought. The vitriol. The latent threat.

Plus the thought that what was at stake here was the future of the entire valley.

'We could have arranged an interview. We probably still will,' the lawyer said. 'But we thought a visit when you weren't expecting us might answer questions faster than any interview.'

'You can't use the video you're making,' Rab said. His voice was mild again now. 'I reiterate, it's not being made with our permission.'

'It could allay our clients' concerns though,' the lawyer said. 'If you can prove you've been living together as a couple there's no more to be said. It may save both you and our clients a costly law suit.'

Rab sighed. He was still holding her tight, the warmth of his arm a silent message. 'Shall we kick them out or shall we just get this over with? My wife and I are indeed married,' he told the lawyers. 'We have nothing to hide. The entire valley will tell you we've been living together for six months. What else do you need to know?'

'Are you sleeping together?' It was the female lawyer, and in her voice was a trace of the belligerence of the young man.

'Of course we are,' Rab said calmly. 'Why wouldn't we?'

'Except we aren't.'

And Mia had found her voice again. She wasn't a wimp. She'd decided that years ago. Harvey had hurt her, intimidated her, made her a total victim. She'd spent years recovering—had she ever really recovered? But these last months, knowing the valley was safe, increasingly knowing that Rab was her friend, had changed something in her.

And how fortunate was it that these people had come this morning? She'd lain in Rab's arms last night and she'd felt amazing.

Formidable.

She'd relapsed a little in the face of the obnoxious Noel's vitriol, but that strength came back now. Rab was still holding her. The memory of his lovemaking—and the way her body had responded—was still with her.

She could face this threat.

If these people were to be admitted into the house they'd find two used bedrooms and that had to be explained.

'We don't sleep together,' she said now. 'Or at least, not very often. But that's not what you're asking. You're asking if we have sex, and yes, indeed we do. But I've been on my own for many years now, and I like my independence. And that includes being able to retreat when my husband snores.' And then she looked directly into the camera and she smiled. 'Ask any couple how they cope when one of them snores like…'

'Oi!' Rab interrupted, indignation personified, but she peeped a smile at him.

'Well, you do,' she said. 'There's no shame.' And she patted his pecs. 'Most guys who are carrying a bit of extra body weight snore, even if it's mostly muscle…'

'Turn that camera off!' Rab demanded, but his eyes were laughing. Laughing at her?

No. Laughing with her. There was a difference.

'So okay, find any woman whose husband snores.' She chuckled. 'Even if only occasionally. Then ask if they'd like a retreat. In this big house, why not?'

'So you're saying you have separate bedrooms?' The female lawyer looked as if she'd discovered a major piece of evidence. Her tone was suddenly excited.

'Yes, we do,' she said blithely, and she tugged out of Rab's arms and turned and gestured inside. 'Want to see?'

'Mia, we don't have to,' Rab said, sounding worried, but there was still the hint of laughter in his eyes. He'd figured what she was doing, even before Mia turned to him and gave him a reassuring nod.

'I know we don't. This visit is impertinent

and probably illegal, but stuff 'em, they want evidence, let's give 'em evidence.' She turned back to the camera. 'You guys agree that you've turned up without warning on a Sunday morning, at a time when most couples could be assumed to be sleeping in?'

'Yes,' the older lawyer said cautiously.

'My husband and I went out last night,' she told them. 'We had a very good time and arrived home late, so we've just woken. Look at us. You agree we haven't had time to stage anything?'

'I imagine that's correct,' the lawyer said grudgingly. 'We made sure you had no warning.'

'So bring your camera inside,' Mia said grandly and gestured inward, and then turned and led the way.

Rab followed, feeling stunned. For the first few minutes he'd played the protector, determined to keep these people out of the house, determined to keep Mia safe. But now it was Mia who was sashaying down the hall as if she owned it.

She reached her bedroom and flung the door open with a flourish, then stepped aside so the two lawyers could enter.

'My domain,' she said grandly. 'My personal retreat.'

The older lawyer stood back, seemingly uncomfortable, but the woman had no such qualms. She walked in and looked around.

Mia had changed little since she'd been here. Indeed, why should she? She'd never intended to stay here past twelve months, and the idea of filling it with her possessions had made her feel uncomfortable. She kept it neat. The bed was starkly made—she was a nurse and she'd been trained in old school discipline—hospital corners, bedcovers without a crease, crisp white pillows plumped every day that now, because no head had dinted them last night, clearly looked as if the bed hadn't been slept in.

There was no mess in the room at all. Not even slippers under the bed—Mia had shoved those on her feet when she'd made a mad rush for her robe. Normally her robe hung behind the door but now there was nothing. There were no photos on the bedside table. No accoutrements except a simple bedside clock and a box of tissues.

It could be anyone's bedroom. It looked as if it was waiting for guests, not a room a woman slept in every night.

Rab was also gazing around for the first time. This was Mia's domain; he hadn't been in here. Its starkness left him cold.

She was staying here, he thought, and the idea was suddenly bleak. She could take her suitcase from the top of the wardrobe and be gone to-morrow, and the house would close against her as if she'd never been here.

Except...the rest of the house gleamed. The rest of the house looked amazing.

She'd been doing it for him?

For the valley, he reminded himself, but then gazed again at the stark room and thought of the gleaming Aga in the kitchen, the sparkling crystals of the chandelier and he thought, no, definitely for him.

'If I had this for a retreat I might have added a bit of pink,' the female lawyer said suddenly, unexpectedly, and Mia flashed her a grin.

'Depends how much you use it. We're only six months in. I expect by the time we reach our golden wedding anniversary this'll be so stuffed with knick-knacks you wouldn't believe. Maybe even a vibrator under the pillow.'

The older lawyer choked. The woman lawyer stared at Mia—and her face, rigid up until now, suddenly cracked into a reluctant smile.

'He has to keep me happy or I'm back in here,' Mia said serenely and then turned and headed down the hall. 'Right, here's the bathroom...'

The grand bathroom was similarly neat, but here the space was shared. Mia, though, had carefully kept her belongings to one end of the wide shelf that ran along the far wall, and Rab used the other.

'You don't share toothpaste then?' the female lawyer asked, but she was starting to sound as if she was enjoying herself. Mia had her onside, Rab thought, stunned.

'And let him decide how to squeeze it? Look at his tube. Squeezed from the top. I ask you...' She gave a theatrical sigh and the lawyer even giggled.

And then... Rab's room. 'Are you sure you want to see this?' Mia asked as they reached the door. She paused, looking a bit embarrassed, but again Rab had the sensation that she was playing for effect.

'Go on,' Rab said wearily, as if he was done with this whole charade. 'Get it over with.'

'As you wish,' Mia said grandly and threw open the door.

And there was all the evidence they needed—and more.

Last night had been...amazing. It had also been very, very messy. The sexual tension between them had been building from the time they'd walked into the restaurant—or maybe it had been building for the whole six months. Regardless, by the time they'd reached home they both knew exactly what they wanted, and they'd wasted no time. The moment she'd said

'I'm sure' Rab had lifted her off her feet, given a curt nod to the sleepy Boris and said, 'You'll have to excuse us, mate. We have things to attend to.'

Boris had, thankfully, gone straight back to sleep, not even vaguely disturbed by the sounds emanating from Rab's bedroom. By this time he regarded Rab as an extension of his tribe, and saw no need to protect his mistress from him.

And his mistress wanted no such protection. Her need to be with him had been as urgent as his had been to take her, and the evidence lay before them now. A trail of their gorgeous evening clothes led across the floor to the bed. Lacy knickers were on the bedside mat—and how had her bra ended up on the lampshade? The bed itself was a mess—the whole scene pictorial evidence of a very good time.

Rab stopped in the doorway, really seeing the mess for the first time. Evidence indeed. And then he looked down at Mia. She was blushing, but she was also smiling, a faint, cat that got the cream smile.

He had the strongest urge to kick these people out now, sweep her up in his arms again and…

Um…no. They'd come this far, they had to see it to the end.

'Do you have to record this?' he growled, and the female lawyer looked apologetic.

'It's the fastest way to allay the fears of our client,' she told him. 'I promise it will never be shared, and as soon as he's satisfied it'll be wiped. We'll also send you a copy so you can check our filming has been...discreet. George and I can swear to what we've seen if required, but I think we've seen enough. Wouldn't you say, George?'

And the middle-aged lawyer's face was almost beetroot. He was backing out of the door, stammering. 'Indeed. We're so sorry. This has made me feel...tawdry. Indeed, it was only that our client insisted that there was no true marriage that we...'

'He didn't think I could have married Mia because I wanted her?' Rab asked mildly, but he couldn't quite suppress anger. He moved to Mia's side again and hugged her. She'd been fabulous. Brave. Bearing all. Or almost all. He looked again at the sliver of lacy panties on the floor and thought that this was a woman who valued her privacy above everything. That she was so exposed...

'I do want her,' he said, holding her close. 'Mia's my wife, in name and in fact. I love her and I'll protect her for ever. You mess with her, and I'll bring every legal force I can muster down on your heads. She's mine and I'll protect my own, no matter what it takes.'

But his words didn't have the effect he'd intended. Or maybe they had with the lawyers, but not with Mia. He felt Mia stiffen. Not much, not enough for the observers to notice, but it was there. She stayed within the hold of his arms but the warmth, the sinking against him, had suddenly changed.

And when she spoke her voice was suddenly strained. 'That's enough,' she said, and it sounded as if each word was forced from her. 'I hope you've seen what you needed to see. Can you go now, please, and let…and let my husband and me get on with our lives.'

Rab saw them to the door and Mia stayed in the bedroom. It was a warm morning but all of a sudden she found herself shivering. The heat of the night had left her. All that was left were echoes.

Rab's words.

'She's mine and I'll protect my own, no matter what it takes.'

And superimposed were words from years ago. Harvey's voice, imprinted into her brain from so long ago.

'She's mine and I keep my own, no matter what it takes.'

They were completely different, she told herself, but she was staring around the room now and she was feeling as if she was staring into an abyss.

How could she have forgotten?

Rab's phone buzzed into life. It was lying on the bedside table. He was still at the front door, talking to the lawyers, no doubt. Telling them more strongly just how 'married' they were. How much she was 'his'.

It was after nine. Time enough for medical calls to come through. Neither of them was on duty, but this was a small place and in an emergency...

She lifted the phone, still staring at the knickers. Still feeling sick.

'Dr Finlay's phone.'

'Mia? Is that you? Did you have a great night?' It was Ewan. The whole hospital had been egging them on last night. The whole hospital would have been cheering if they could see those knickers.

'Yes,' she said, and she knew her voice sounded flat. 'Thank you.'

There was a moment's silence. He knew her well, the old doctor. Then, 'Is everything okay?'

'I...' She struggled to pull herself together. 'Yes. Sorry. We've just had a visit from lawyers wanting to prove we're properly married.' She might as well tell him, she thought. The whole valley would have noticed a sleek black car heading for their place at this hour on a Sunday.

'That's why you sound strained,' Ewan said, sounding relieved. 'I imagine you reassured them.'

'We sure did.' And she struggled to put a smile behind her words. 'I guess…they're just leaving now.'

'That's great,' he told her. 'But, Mia…'

Here we go, she thought. Medicine.

'John and Miranda Hutchins celebrated their fortieth wedding anniversary last night,' Ewan told her. 'Half the valley was there, and their daughters catered. Apparently they've been making casseroles for weeks. Put 'em in hired bain-maries, kept them warm all day. We had John come in at four this morning with food poisoning, and a steady stream of locals have been phoning for advice or arriving since. Most are minor but a couple of the oldies have been hit hard. You reckon you and Rab could stop playing married for a bit and come in and help?'

Playing married… The words had been said almost as a joke. Ewan thought of them as truly married.

Playing married…

She stared at the knickers again and thought of how out of control she'd been last night. She

thought of every vow she'd ever made since...
well, since Harvey.

'She's mine.'

She wasn't. The façade had to continue for
another six months, but that was all it was. A
façade.

'We'll be there as soon as possible,' she said
tersely and disconnected. Then she took a
deep breath, gathered her scattered clothes and
headed for her room.

By the time Rab returned from seeing the
lawyers off she was in the bathroom, in the
shower, with the door locked behind her.

'Mia?' he called from outside the door and
she heard concern. 'Are you okay?'

'We're wanted at the hospital,' she called
back. 'Food poisoning, multiple presentations.
Bathroom's yours in two minutes.'

The door was locked. The way she'd been
feeling last night, she would have left it open.
They could have showered together.

She's mine.

She wasn't. The door was staying locked until
she was safely back in her part of the house.

Back in control.

Back being Mia.

Somehow he'd messed it up and there didn't
seem a thing he could do about it. He knew

from the moment he'd heard her voice from the bathroom that the barriers had been put in place again.

In the car on the way to the hospital he tried to raise it. 'Mia, I'm so sorry they upset you.'

'They didn't upset me,' she said tightly. 'It was lucky that last night happened when it did.'

'It was lucky,' he said. And then, more cautiously, 'It was wonderful.'

'Yep.' But her voice was tight.

'Not for you?'

'Yes.' Then, more tightly still, 'No. I forgot my rules. This is a pretend marriage, Rab. Six more months and we're done.'

'Does it have to be a pretend marriage?' He was driving, needing to focus on the road. Maybe this conversation should have waited until tonight, but she seemed wound so tight, as if she'd…betrayed herself.

'Mia,' he said, gently now, 'you sound horrified. I'm not Harvey, Mia. You know I'd never hurt you. You know I'd protect you with everything I possess and more.'

'I don't want to be protected.'

'You don't want to be loved?'

'I…no.'

'I didn't think I did either,' he said, almost conversationally, although he was struggling to get the words out. 'But, Mia, you've been so battered, you're so vulnerable. I know the façade you wear, how hard it must have been to build that, but I can see past it. Couldn't you learn to let yourself love?'

'You mean, let myself need?'

'Maybe,' he said softly. 'Would it be so hard to lean on me? Would it be so hard to let me in?'

'I can't.' She said it harshly.

'You mean you can't trust me?'

'I do trust you. I just can't let myself need you. I want control, Rab.'

'You have control.'

'I don't. I lost it last night. I've got it back now and I'm not letting it go.'

'So you and me…'

'You might want me,' she said, softly now, staring straight ahead at the winding river as they approached the hospital. 'But you're still as independent as you always were. But me… Rab, if I went further down the road we went last night then I'd lose myself. I would need you and that'd make me so vulnerable I couldn't bear it. You said to those people, "She's mine". I'm not, Rab, I never was and I never will be. You're special and I know you'd care for me, but that's not what I want. I just…'

She bit back her words and closed her eyes. He was slowing to turn into the hospital car park. Medicine was waiting, a way for both of them to switch off personal emotion, to immerse themselves in a world where there was no room for personal reflection. He knew, suddenly, that this was his last chance. She'd climb out of the car, head back into her world and the emotional door would be closed behind him.

'Mia, I think I love you.' He said it a bit too loudly.

'You said that during the night,' she said flatly, her hand on the door. 'It's what people say during...'

'Did Harvey say it to you?'

'Probably. I can't remember. It doesn't mean anything.'

'Mia...'

'Leave it, Rab,' she said wearily. 'Last night was an aberration. It was fortunate it happened at the right time to convince the lawyers, but that's all we should remember it as. A one-night stand with lucky repercussions for the valley, but nothing else. Now...'. She pushed the door wide and climbed out. 'Let's get back to work. Food poisoning, here we come.'

CHAPTER TWELVE

Harvey was out of prison.

It was three months on from 'the night of the lawyers'. That was how she'd labelled the restaurant meal and everything that had happened that night, categorising it in her mind as a lucky incident that had cemented the valley's safety for ever. She even somehow tried to rewrite it in her head as a strategic move, something they might have staged.

She couldn't quite get there, but if she blanked out the time from when they'd left the restaurant to the time the lawyers had knocked on the door then she managed to keep it in some sort of perspective. The time in between she left locked away, a memory so vivid she couldn't let it out of the bomb-proof compartment she'd formed in her head.

She had many such compartments. One of them was Harvey, and now, staring at the letter in her hand, she felt it being wedged open.

The parole board had accepted his application, the letter told her. As the victim of his crime, this was a courtesy letter. The letter had been sent via a redirecting service she'd set up when she'd changed her name. This letter was two weeks old.

He'd never find her anyway, she thought, fighting a wash of panic that he'd been out without her knowing. Part of his parole conditions was not to go anywhere near her, but even if he tried, she'd moved to this valley then changed her name again when she'd married Rab. Mia Finlay had nothing to do with the terrified Maira of ten years ago.

She was no longer a victim. Harvey was nothing to do with her. This letter was nothing to do with her.

'Mia? Is something wrong?'

They were eating breakfast, seated on opposite sides of the table, getting ready for work. Reading their respective news feeds and mail. Keeping separate.

She'd headed out early for a walk with Boris and had collected the mail from the post box at the end of the drive on the way back. It was her routine.

Routine was everything now. Since...the night of the lawyers...they'd maintained a formality not usually even seen between housemates. It was as if each of them knew that the chasm was there waiting, one chink and they'd fall.

Into lust?

Cut it out, she told herself savagely, and she made it savage because the concern in Rab's voice was enough to threaten the fragile barriers she fought so hard to defend.

'Nothing,' she said briefly, and laid down the letter. And then, because it wasn't enough to just set it aside, she rose, took it over to the fire stove and set it to burn. 'Just…my ex-husband's out of jail.'

His face stilled. 'Mia…'

'It's okay. He's nothing to do with me now. Nothing at all.' But her voice trembled. Dammit, why? He was no threat. She was not that girl any more. Not that woman.

'Do you think he'll try to find you?'

And for some reason that calmed her, his steady voice cutting across her panic. It was a reasonable question and it forced her into logic.

'There's no reason why he should. It's ten years ago now.'

'Was the assault on you the only thing that put him in jail?'

Once again, she was steadied by the matter-of-factness in his tone.

'Drug charges as well,' she managed. 'And

firearms. When the police came…after the assault…they found a lot of them.'

'So there's no reason he'll have been sitting in jail all this time thinking his sentence is your fault?'

Her eyes flashed to his. There it was—the unspoken fear. He got it, she thought. He understood.

And suddenly Harvey's voice was echoing in her head, as it had echoed for years. They'd set up a screen in the rehab department so she could watch the trial. It was something she should do, the psychologists had told her. 'You need to hear the judge saying what a scumbag he really is. This should help you acknowledge, once and for all, that nothing about this is your fault.'

And maybe they were right, but what she was left with was an image, Harvey screaming up at the camera as if he could see her behind the lens.

'I'll come for you… No matter where you are, no matter how long it takes. You're mine.'

She shuddered and all at once Rab was standing, taking her hands, pulling her up and against his chest. And just for a moment she let herself be pulled. She let herself sink against his sweater, feel the scratch of thick wool, feel the strength of him, the safety…

'You're safe, Mia,' he said firmly, surely. 'I won't let him hurt you.'

And there were the echoes again. He'd protect her?

You're mine.

Whoa. She was being stupid, she knew she was, but she didn't need this man's protection. She couldn't. She'd carefully constructed her life so she depended on no one, and there was no way she'd sink back into that helplessness. She pulled back and took a couple of deep breaths.

'Thanks, but I don't need it,' she told him.

'You don't need me?'

'I can't need you.' She tilted her chin and met his look square-on. 'I can't need anyone. Can't you see that?'

'I guess... I can't.'

'I'm sorry, but I can't explain it any better than that,' she said, and dammit, her voice was bleak. 'And I know you'd protect me, as I know this whole valley'd protect me, and Boris too, for that matter. So I'm safe, but you know what? I'm safe because of my choices, because of my strengths. So thank you for the hug, Rab. It helped and I'll add it to my arsenal, but now... moving on, I have antenatal classes in the school hall in half an hour and I need to move. We both need to move. The letter's burned and forgotten. Let's go.'

* * *

She left, driving in her little Mini, leaving him to follow. He watched her go and felt...bad. He couldn't define it any better than that.

Was he afraid for her? Maybe, but her assurance had been firm.

Did he want her to need him? Maybe.

He raked his fingers through his hair and swore and then turned to Boris. 'Come on. I don't have patients until ten and I'm sure you need another walk.'

Boris looked at him as if he was nuts. He'd obviously done a few kilometres with Mia. He was getting on in dog years. The fire was warm.

'Come on,' Rab told him. 'I need company.'

And then he heard what he'd said.

I need...

Mia didn't need him.

That long-ago line was suddenly playing in his head. *'I need this woman so much—I'm just so lucky she needs me right back.'*

Mia didn't need him, but hell, the way he was feeling...

Was it possible that the tables had turned?

The day turned out busy, more than busy. Some days there was just one thing after another. At five, just as Mia was due to knock off, she heard the dreaded screech of tyres, a car speeding up to the entrance, a car door slamming, a female voice yelling for assistance.

'Help! Help me, please! My husband…'

An accident? Ewan had gone home early. Night staff were about to take over, but both Rab and Mia were there. They headed out together, bracing as they always did.

Donald Myers, a big, beefy farmer from up in the hill country, was sprawled in the passenger seat, gasping for air. His face was puffy, the hand he held to his chest was swollen. He was red-faced, sweating, and his eyes were wide with terror.

'He's just… Half an hour ago… He just started to swell.' Kath Myers was a sensible woman, a stalwart in the Country Women's Association, maker of the best scones in the valley. When fires had threatened the town three years ago she'd been the calmest of them all, but there was nothing calm about her now.

'He can't breathe,' she managed. 'He can't even talk any more. Mia, help…'

'Intubation,' Rab snapped, crouching to the level of the guy in the car. 'Don, hey, this looks like an allergic reaction. Scary, but we have you.' Then back to Mia. 'Epinephrine, methyl prednisolone and prepare to intubate. Don, we're going to get you out of trouble, we'll get the swelling down, but first things first, we need to help you breathe.'

He was tearing Don's shirt. Mia was already moving, grabbing the crash cart from just inside the doorway, motioning Issy to bring the trolley. For the first few moments there was no time for questions, no time to do anything but get him out of the car, get the epinephrine aboard, then get him sedated enough to intubate. This was a procedure so drilled into all of them that there was no need to speak, no need for anything but to use what was almost muscle memory to keep the man alive.

But Mia's mind was racing as she worked. This was no normal allergic reaction. She'd known Don for years now, a no-nonsense farmer who pretty much spent all his time on his land. At this time of the evening, on a weekday, he'd hardly have been out at a restaurant, and Kath was known for good, plain cooking. So what?

He kept bees on his property. 'Has he been near the hives?' she asked over her shoulder. Kath was standing in the background, looking terrified. By rights they should have had a social worker or at least a junior who'd accompany her to the waiting room, who'd sit with her, but right now there were only Mia, Rab and Issy on duty, and they were all needed.

'I'm staying with him,' Kath had declared as

they'd wheeled him inside and there'd been no time to argue. In truth, it was probably kinder to let her stay rather than make her sit alone.

'Not since last week,' Kath stammered. 'And he doesn't react to bee stings. He's been bitten so many times in the past, it doesn't worry him.'

'So today, anything out of the ordinary?'

'The dentist?' The woman took a deep breath. She also had obviously been fighting to make sense of what was happening. 'He's had tooth-ache. We went across to Colambool this morn-ing. The dentist there said he has an abscess. She didn't have time to work on it today, she said come back on Wednesday. She gave him antibiotics.'

'What sort?' Rab snapped, suddenly focused on Kath.

'I don't know,' the woman faltered. 'A green… a green bottle. White pills.'

'Has he had an allergic reaction in the past?'

'No. He never gets sick. He never…'

'It's okay. We'll get through this.' Mia was handing Rab equipment. The anaesthetic he'd administered—mostly tranquilliser to stop the gag reflex—was taking effect and Rab had the intubation tube ready. 'Issy—' she talked over her shoulder '—ring the dental clinic at Colambool. If it's closed, if no one's answering, then ring the police station. They'll be able to track down someone who can access the dentist's records. Tell them it's an emergency. We need to know what was prescribed and we need to know now. Fast!'

The girl turned and fled. She was good, was Issy. She knew the locals—she'd probably be able to track the dentist down herself.

The tube was sliding home, and the moment it did Don's desperate efforts to breathe pretty much eased. The hiss of the air through the tube was a comfort. Standing by the wall, Kath almost visibly slumped.

'Oh, thank God. Oh, my…is it the antibiotic?'

'Most likely,' Mia told her and then glanced at Rab. With the immediate danger past they had a little time. 'Let's make you a cup of tea and ring your daughters to come and join you. You've had a fright and you need company. Oh, and you might ask one of them to stop at your place and pack Don's PJs and toothbrush.'

'Will he need to stay the night?'

Mia's gaze flew to Rab's. Their eyes met and she knew that her guess—that this was no minor reaction, something major was happening—was spot-on.

'Certainly tonight,' she told her. 'It'll take a while for the swelling to go down.'

And then Issy was back in the room. 'There was still someone in the clinic,' she told them.

'Not the dentist—she's a locum there while Marjorie Chambers is on holiday—and she'd gone home for the day. But there was a dental nurse catching up on something. She looked at the records. Penicillin.'

There was a moment's stillness. Anaphylaxis caused by penicillin was as rare as hen's teeth, but the potential consequences were appalling. There was a reason doctors asked for medical history when they prescribed drugs, and this was a major one. Breathing difficulties could be the least of it.

'That's great,' Rab said, but the look he gave Mia said it all. It wasn't great at all, but there was no use terrifying Kath any more. Not now. 'Issy, could you take Kath for her cup of tea? Mia, I need you to keep an eye on this tube for a bit.' He sent an apologetic glance to Kath. 'You've come at a busy time, and I need to make a couple of phone calls.'

The medevac chopper landed in the paddock behind the hospital at eight that night. Two paramedics were aboard. No doctor. 'There wasn't anyone available,' they'd told Rab.

Rab had only seen such an allergic reaction once in his medical career before. It had been a child. He still couldn't bear thinking about it.

He knew he had to go on the chopper.

'There's a real risk of heart failure,' he told Mia and Ewan. Ewan had arrived back at the hospital within half an hour of Don's arrival—this valley had ears.

'Yeah,' Ewan agreed. 'Rhonda's gone to their place with one of the daughters, packing stuff for Kath. Kath'll go with him too, but the kids'll go by car. I told them it might take a few days. Maybe by a miracle he'll come out of it fast but… Anyway, Rab, I agree, you need to go too.'

He didn't need to say any more.

Mia had seen this reaction once before too. An older woman. It had taken her months to recover.

They were busy, trying to stabilise Don, trying to think of every eventuality, every medical crisis Rab could face in the hour-long journey.

And then they were gone and suddenly Mia felt like slumping into the nearest chair and weeping.

It was this valley, she thought. It had protected her, saved her, and its inhabitants felt like part of her. To lose one of them… No.

And now she'd go home tonight without Rab. He was flying back to Sydney—where he belonged. He'd come back, she knew he would, but only for another three months.

Unless…

Dammit, why were these emotions surfacing now?

'Go home.' Ewan was watching her face. He knew her well, this man. He'd seen her almost at her worst and she could hardly hide things from him now. 'Would you like one of us to come and stay the night with you? It's a bit lonely, staying in that big house by yourself.'

He saw too much, did Ewan. He was watching her and she knew darn well he wasn't thinking she was spooked by a big house. But that she'd miss…her husband.

Her pretend husband, she told herself fiercely. Pretend.

'Hey, we've been in and out of that house while we've been on call any time these last nine months,' she said, managing a smile. 'I'm not dependent…'

'On anything or anyone. I get that.' His smile was infinitely gentle. 'And that's a problem I was starting to hope Rab had fixed. But it's okay,' he added as he saw her flinch. 'There's time. And meanwhile you have Boris. Go home and hug your dog, girl. Don'll be okay, Rab will see to that. You can trust him, lass. You really can.'

'I know I can,' she said, and kept her smile determinedly fixed. 'Thanks, Ewan. Goodnight.'

And she went out to the car park and headed for home.

Home?

Home is where the heart is. The trite little saying started playing over and over in her head as she drove. So…home?

Maybe home was in a helicopter, somewhere in the night sky. Heading for Sydney.

Why did he hate leaving her tonight?

It was the news she'd told him at breakfast, her expression. She was terrified.

He was totally caught up with Don's care. He and the paramedics were throwing every ounce of their combined skill at preserving vital signs, when the sheer force of the reaction to the antibiotic was doing the exact opposite.

But still there was a tiny part of his brain that was telling him he should have told Ewan about Harvey's release, urged her to stay with him, maybe urged Rhonda or Joanne or Issy to stay with her tonight.

Which was stupid. Firstly, the guy had only just got out of prison. Even if he was intent on revenge, Mia was right, she'd protected herself well. It'd take time and effort to find her.

And, secondly, he knew exactly how she would have reacted if he'd suggested it.

'I'm safe because of my choices, because of my strengths.'

Her voice still echoed in his head, telling him to butt out.

But she did need him. He could see it in her reaction, in the way she'd folded into him for the hug. And he wanted her to need him. He ached for it.

Why couldn't she see that it was no weakness? That it'd be his privilege to take care of her for the rest of her life.

And then Don's body gave a convulsive jerk and he glanced at the monitors. His heart... This was what they most feared.

The thought of Mia disappeared, or almost disappeared, as every fibre of his medical self fought to keep the guy alive. Don needed him, right here, right now. Mia, not so much.

The fact that he wanted her to need him?

Put it away, he told himself. The thought of Mia folded against his chest this morning had to be put aside.

For now. There had to be a future, he told himself.

Please.

She pulled up outside the darkened homestead and let herself sit for a moment. The silence enveloped her. Home.

Home without Rab?

Yeah, well, she was used to it. During the last nine months she and Rab had worked as medics, sometimes together, often apart. They'd both had calls that hadn't involved the other. They were used to coming home alone.

So why was she sitting in the car now, not wanting to go in?

Because the parole board had written her a letter.

Because Rab wouldn't be here.

Both those things were irrelevant. They had nothing to do with her. 'You've spent the last ten years finding independence and control,' she muttered to herself. 'Don't falter at the first hurdle.'

Was Rab a hurdle?

He certainly threatened her independence. She thought of how she'd felt this morning, hugged against his sweater. Safe. Protected.

Stupid.

But he wanted her to need him. She could see that. He'd like nothing better than to protect her for the rest of her life.

Which would make her feel small. She could hardly understand it herself, the sensation of falling she had when she was with him. The desire to be his, and yet the fierce determination to be nobody's.

Maybe she should ring her therapist again. *Hey, Lorna, I have this gorgeous hunk who wants to love and protect me for the rest of my life.*

But she knew what Lorna would say. *Mia, is this another shield against the world?*

Maybe it was, and she didn't need it.

Oh, for heaven's sake, she was emotional and tired and Boris was inside, probably aching for a walk. It'd have to be a quick one tonight, though, she thought. Maybe she could pour herself a glass of wine, sit on the steps and tell him to romp in the front paddock. There were enough rabbits down there to keep him happy.

Do it, she told herself and climbed from the car.

She opened the front door, expecting Boris to come hurtling to greet her.

'Boris?'

Nothing.

And with that the shadows came flooding back, a fear so overwhelming it made her stagger—even before the door closed behind her and hands gripped and held.

Before something jabbed hard into her thigh.

Before the hold on her tightened still further.

Before the gasping struggle for breath.

Before blackness.

CHAPTER THIRTEEN

HE FLEW BACK at dawn.

He was exhausted. He'd been awake most of the night and there'd been an offer to stay on and get a decent sleep at Sydney Central. Which would have been sensible.

But Don was in the best of hands. It'd take time for him to recover from such a massive allergic reaction, but he was in the Intensive Care Unit in one of the best hospitals in the world. He had his wife with him. His daughters were driving up from the valley this morning. There was every chance he'd make a full recovery. There was nothing more for Rab to do. When the medevac operator rang and said there was a flight leaving from dawn to pick someone up from Colambool and offering him a lift, there seemed no choice.

He wanted to be home.

The chopper crew—a different team from the one who'd flown the night before—were friendly and accommodating. They checked the paddock in front of Wiradjuri and saw no reason why they shouldn't set him down there, and two minutes after he landed he was opening the front door.

Which wasn't locked.

Mia must have taken Boris for an early walk, he thought, but then he heard an urgent scratching from further down the passage.

He headed for the kitchen, opened the door and Boris almost knocked him over in his joy to be out. But three quick licks and the dog was gone, hurtling down the passage and out into the yard. He was clearly heading to do what a well-trained dog would never allow himself to do on the kitchen floor.

Rab stared after him, feeling…as if the floor was shaking under him.

'Mia?' His first call was tentative. His next was almost a shout, and he'd turned and was at Mia's bedroom door before he realised it.

The room was empty, the bed was made. The room looked impersonal. Well, what was new? She'd never made it homelike, he thought tangentially.

She didn't feel that she belonged here.

She wasn't here now. If it wasn't for Boris he might have thought…

No. Her suitcase was on top of the wardrobe.

He tugged the wardrobe doors open and her clothes were still lined up.

She could have gone to work early, but Boris… Why had Boris been locked in?

He headed back to the hall, kicking open the bathroom door as he went. Just in case.

In case what? That she'd collapsed? Had an accident?

He headed outside. Boris bounded back to greet him, welcoming him like a long-lost friend.

The Mini was still here.

Where…?

He turned and stared inside, and then he saw what he hadn't noticed as he'd gone in the first time. On the sitting room floor, looking as if it had been kicked from across from the hall, lay her purse. Three strides and he was kneeling, hauling it open.

Her phone was inside.

And then he saw the empty syringe.

His heart felt as if it had been clutched by icy fingers. No!

He went to lift it, then had enough forethought to grab an antimacassar from the back of one of his grandfather's chairs. He used it to lift the syringe, holding it to the light. He saw the remains of a clear substance. He squeezed and lifted it to his nose.

Nothing.

Phenobarb? Morphine? That was his surgical training kicking in.

Heroin? Much more likely.

But any of those options made his heart clench. If this syringe had been full, then no matter what it was, it was more than enough to knock out someone a lot larger than Mia.

And side effects were blazing in his head. Irregular heartbeat. Low blood pressure.

Death.

Dear God, if this was Harvey... If he'd administered the drug by force...

It was all he could do not to throw up, but that'd help no one. He forced himself to breathe slowly, staying very still, forcing his mind back from dread.

How long ago had this happened? Where would he have taken her?

Could she be dead?

He couldn't think it. Not for a moment.

Boris came in and sat beside him, looking puzzled, putting his great head forward so he could lick his face.

Strangely, the sensation of the dog's rasping tongue against his cheek helped. Boris was looking at him as if he was the one to pull them out of this nightmare.

So do something.

Police.

He grabbed his phone and the local cop answered on the second ring. Brian was a friend of Mia's. Everyone was a friend of Mia's.

'I'll be there in two minutes. Don't touch anything,' he growled, and the phone went dead.

What next?

Somehow he forced his dazed mind to think. If he'd meant to kill her, surely he would have done it here. So surely he wanted her alive? He didn't know that for certain, but anything else was unthinkable.

So he wanted her alive, but not here?

Somewhere.

Think!

And then he had it, a sliver of memory from a long-ago conversation.

'Harvey lived in a huge house at the bottom of the district's only hill...'

And... *'I bet it's still his. It was sold when he went to jail but one of his mates bought it, and I'm betting he'll end up back there.'*

Where had she said it was?

Corduna.

He grabbed his phone and did a search. Corduna. Three hours away by road.

There had to be somewhere else. He surely wouldn't take her all that way, drugged, unconscious.

Dead?

He couldn't want her dead, he told himself again, clinging desperately to that hope. If he wanted to kill her, he never would have bothered with drugs. No, he'd want vengeance first, he thought, a way to punish her for ten years of prison.

Boris had sat back on his haunches, head cocked to the side, obviously puzzled that Rab was still on his knees, staring into middle distance. He grabbed the dog and hugged him, and Boris obliged by putting his huge head into his chest and nuzzling. It was pretty much a cuddle of comfort.

It was Mia who needed the cuddle, he thought savagely. It was Mia who needed him.

Where was Brian? There was nothing he could do until the police arrived. He had to sit still and wait.

He held the dog tight against him, using his warmth, the solid trust of him, to catch himself, to regroup, to figure that he could stand up, head out to the veranda, meet Brian, figure a plan.

He had to get to Mia. Mia needed him.

And then, as he held Boris tighter, as the dog's raspy tongue found his cheek again, he thought suddenly, stupidly, that he needed Boris.

And it was as if a chink in his heart was suddenly being crowbarred open. He needed the dog's presence. He needed…

He needed Mia.

This way he was feeling… He had to get to Mia, rescue her, save her, but it wasn't all about Mia's need. He needed her to be where Boris was right now. He needed her against his heart.

He'd told Mia he wanted to marry her to protect her, to love her, to keep her safe. She needed him, of course she did. But now…

He closed his eyes as the wash of self-knowledge grew so great it threatened to overwhelm him.

Somewhere out there was the woman he loved.

Somewhere out there was the woman he needed more than life itself.

It wasn't Mia's need, it was his.

Somewhere out there was…his home.

She woke to blackness. She woke to absolute confusion.

She felt sick, fuzzy, weird. The world seemed to be spinning around her. Nothing made sense. She wanted, badly, to be sick. There were no lights, or maybe there were but they were intermittent. Flash, nothing, nothing, nothing, flash, nothing, flash…

The only thing she could do was to focus

quite hard on not throwing up, and it took pretty much every ounce of self-discipline she had. For some reason it felt vitally important not to vomit. To retch alone in the darkness… The indignity as well as the mess… She wouldn't do it. And overriding everything else was the age-old instinct of wounded creatures, to lie still, to stay hidden until they knew the threat.

And the threat was suddenly with her. Slivers of memory were returning.

She lay still, fighting for control of her body and fighting for control of panic as images flooded back.

Harvey. His great body looming over her. Hands holding her down, turning her face to the floor.

A jab… Then nothing.

Drugs. He'd drugged her.

Of course. Once upon a time Harvey had had the means to get any drug he wanted. He'd just come out of prison, but he'd still have contacts on the outside.

He'd used something on her. What?

It didn't make sense. Nothing made sense. She had to get rid of the fog.

There was no choice but to close her eyes and give herself space, to fight the nausea, to fight the panic. She needed to let the fog envelop her until whatever he'd drugged her with wore off.

Darkness. Nothing, nothing, flash.

They were in a car! The moment she thought it, it made sense. The vinyl feel against her cheek. The sense of movement. The flash of passing cars.

They were travelling fast. Where? And how long had she been unconscious?

There was nothing she could do. She wasn't tied, but they were travelling too fast for her to try and escape, even if the doors weren't locked. She was too fuzzy to move anyway but, even if she wasn't, survival instinct was still screaming at her to not let whoever else was in the car sense that she was coming round.

She didn't feel like coming round. Oh, she felt sick.

She wanted…oh, she wanted…

Rab.

The memory of *The Wind in the Willows* was suddenly with her, the story she'd read over and over in the past years. It was her place of peace and she could use it now.

Her eyes stayed firmly closed and with a conscious effort she let the memory of Rab's voice take over.

"'The Mole was bewitched, entranced, fascinated. By the side of the river he trotted as one trots, when very small…'"

Rab's voice with that long-ago reading was

suddenly with her, whispering into her poor foggy head, helping her fight back fear.

Where are you, love? She could almost hear herself say it. The question was nonsensical. She was on her own, she always had been.

But it helped. Somewhere out in the world was Rab and he'd be frightened with her.

And Boris.

And Mole.

She almost smiled, but then another wave of nausea swept over her.

Close your eyes, she told herself. Let yourself sink back into the fog but don't let it frighten you.

Mole. The river.

Rab.

'We're doing all we can.' Brian looked as if he was having trouble staying calm himself. 'We have roadblocks all over the valley. We're contacting the prison, finding associates, trying to find what car he's driving. He's been out of jail for two weeks but he should be reporting in. We'll find out where he's been living. It's just…'

It was seven in the morning and they'd be waking officials and it'd take time. And all that time Mia would be lying in some brute's car, or taken into some motel or refuge they didn't know about or…or…

He was going nuts.

'What about Corduna?'

'Three hours away by car, mate, and we don't even know if he still has a house there. But we're checking. There's no police based there—Corduna's more a hamlet than a town—but they'll send people.'

'How long will that take?'

'An hour maybe, apparently it's bloody rough country.'

'I need to go there.'

'You're best to stay here.'

'Why the hell?'

'In case she comes home.' The big cop stirred uneasily, and Rab had the feeling that, like him, he wanted to be out and doing something. 'Mate, this is a kidnapping. You're family. You gotta sit it out. We both do. We have people working on it now, guys who know their stuff.'

'But she can't come home. She's drugged and Corduna's our only link. And we have no idea how long she's been gone. Corduna... I need to get there.'

'Doc, we're doing our best and we have no evidence...'

'Okay, you have no evidence,' Rab said explosively. 'But it's our only lead and if he takes her there...can you get the air guys in? Choppers from Sydney?'

'Not yet. They'll need more evidence showing that's where he's taken her. The ground guys will work on that.'

He was losing his mind. He had to do something. 'I'm going.'

'Drive for three hours to a place we don't even know he still owns? Who's to say he hasn't taken her to a motel down the road?'

'He'd want her on his own turf.' The vision of Harvey's retreat, vividly described by Mia, was in his head. Barbed wire, dogs, a compound where he could do what he liked with her. Thoughts were flashing through his head, a kaleidoscope of fear and plans and visions of Mia being... Mia being...

'Tom,' he said suddenly. 'His helicopter. He'll take me.'

'Tom?'

'You know, Tom Cray. He has a chopper. He takes people for a fee. Can you contact him?'

'Hell, mate...'

'Brian, this is Mia. Mia!'

And the cop stood still and stared at him. Mia seemed such an integral part of this community, and Rab could see emotion warring with protocol and sense.

'You gotta stay here,' he said at last. 'Rules. Family stays home. If we find her, you gotta be here.'

'Brian, she's drugged and gone. What are the chances she'll be returned here?'

'If the roadblocks work…'

'How many roads lead in and out of this place? And how long have they been gone? There's a dribble of drug on the carpet and it's dry. I have to go. If it's against rules…arrest me if you must, because that's the only way you can stop me.'

'Not by yourself. And Tom'd be useless…if there was trouble.'

'Then come with me yourself.'

The cop stared at him, indecision warring with protocol.

'This is Mia,' Rab said, softly now. 'You've seen the scars on her face. That's how badly he hurt her last time he had her.'

And he watched as slowly the big cop thought of Mia, thought of the scars. Made a decision.

'Hell,' he said savagely. 'Okay, you ring Tom. I'll get a couple of locals to head out here and look out for this place, just in case she gets back.' He shrugged. 'It's probably needle in a haystack stuff, but if Tom can take us…let's do it.'

All she wanted was Rab.

How dumb was that? She should be thinking

all she wanted was freedom, all she wanted was to be free of Harvey, all she wanted was safety.

Instead she lay on the rough cloth of a settee and let herself drift back into the sensations she'd felt in Rab's bed.

That was a good place to be. No, it was amazing. It was the only way she could distract herself—and she needed to be distracted.

From the time she'd surfaced to something akin to consciousness, survival instincts had kicked in. She'd had no way of getting out of the car, no way of escaping Harvey, not unless she could figure out some way she had the advantage—and there was no way she could get that advantage while she was still half drugged.

So she lay and played dead. Even when the car pulled up, when she heard gates creak open, when she heard the dogs and knew for certain where she was and that the gates would close behind her, she didn't make a move. If she got to the door, if she tried to run, the dogs would be on her in moments.

Her stomach was still heaving, and when he picked her up and dumped her unceremoniously on the settee in the living room, then shook her, trying to rouse her, the smell of him, the feel of him, was the last straw. As he tried to haul her upright she retched, but then, as every instinct screamed to fight him, to haul away, she forced herself to slump back, limp, seemingly unconscious.

She heard his grunt of disgust. 'You'll wait,' he growled and she heard him stomp back into the kitchen.

She heard him on the phone. 'Yeah, mate, I got her here. Still out of it—how was I to know how much to give her? Thanks for keeping the place for me. Dogs were no problem, I let 'em out as soon as we arrived. They'll be no problem when we leave—amazing what a bit of steak'll do and you've left us plenty. I coulda done with whisky instead of beer, but you can drop it in later. I won't be in a hurry leaving.' And he gave a mirthless laugh and disconnected.

She lay absolutely still. She had to figure this out and she only had this time to do it.

She had to get control. Now, before this 'mate' arrived.

Strangely, lying on the foul settee, feigning unconsciousness, she felt herself regrouping. She wasn't the woman who'd been so helpless all those years ago. Harvey had caught her unawares and brought her here, but she wasn't *that* woman.

She was in control, she told herself. She just had to figure out how.

* * *

The chopper flew through the early morning sky, going two, three times as fast as a car but still not fast enough for Rab.

The local cops would meet them there, but it had taken strings to make that happen.

'The victim's husband's going anyway, whether we like it or not, and I need to go with him.' Brian had stuck to his story, even though the response from the guys on the ground had been less than enthusiastic.

'Harvey's place was sold when he went to prison. We have no idea who the new owner is. Are you suggesting we storm the place?'

'He's going anyway,' Brian told them, stone-walling their objections.

So was it a wild goose chase? He was in a chopper heading for a place that Harvey hadn't owned for years. There were so many other places he could take her. It didn't make sense.

Except his gut said it did.

And Mia's words. *'It was his own private kingdom... I sometimes think that most of his vitriol towards me in the trial was because finally I caused the authorities to breach his defences.'*

So he had to be right. He must. This was Mia. Dear God, if she was hurt... If he lost her.

Something inside him would die, he thought.

He didn't need to save her for her sake. He needed to save her for his.

She had a plan. There were holes but it was the best she could do. She had one chance, she told herself, and she'd use it. One chance...

She'd trained for this. She had the skills.

So use them.

He was approaching again. She felt herself tense, and had to consciously force herself to limpness again, so that when he walked to where she lay and shook her she reacted as if she were a bunch of rags.

He swore.

Turn away, she pleaded with him under her breath. Turn your back.

How often had she rehearsed this move? 'It's the most effective for total disablement,' her karate instructor had told her. 'But you need to be behind him.' He'd taught her other moves for frontal contact, but she was so much smaller than he was. She knew one false slip and the thing would end in disaster. This was her best chance.

It had to work.

I will be in control, she told herself. It was a mantra. Her mantra. Given to her by Rab all those years ago.

'That's okay, Maira... You're in control.'

Rab. The thought of him somehow settled the panic within. He was out there somewhere. He loved her.

It shouldn't matter. She didn't need him, but it helped.

She had to do this now. Now!

She stayed limp as he shook her again. He swore and let her fall back on the cushions. 'Bloody stuff... If he's given too much...'

She felt rather than saw him turn away, and finally she let her body tense. If he tried to lift her now she'd be rigid. Coiled like a cobra about to strike. Ready.

Now!

And all those years of self-defence classes actually worked. Robyn, her social worker, had been adamant that she should do them. 'You'll never need them, but they'll help the way you feel. Maira, you've been treated as a doormat all your life. Now it's time to learn your own strength.'

Her karate teacher had seen her scars, learned her background and taught accordingly.

'Here's the nice stuff,' he'd told her. 'It'll teach you all the movements. But here's the dirty stuff, the stuff you only ever use if you're intent on major hurt.'

Which was what she used now. Go!

She flew up from the couch, using her coiled strength, not staggering, covering the tiny distance between them like a well-aimed arrow, giving him no time to turn.

He sensed. He started to twist. He was almost side on…

She raised her knee and she kicked straight out, viciously, using all her strength and more, so the heel of her foot slammed into the back of his knee.

This was a *yoko geri* side kick and it was designed to rip ligaments. It was not to be thought of in any but the most dire situation, but that situation was now.

And it worked. He screamed and dropped, but even before he hit the ground she was on him. She had his arms behind him, pushing them up so hard he kept right on screaming.

In those blessed moments where she'd lain, feigning unconsciousness, she'd figured a plan. She wore clogs at work, plastic things that were easy to wash. They'd dropped off somewhere on the journey, but underneath she wore light socks that reached halfway up her calves. Thin, stretchy socks. She'd surreptitiously pushed them down to her ankles, and it took milliseconds to grasp them now.

She used one for his wrists, using the same

method her mother had taught her to tie legs on a roast chicken, trussing hard, tight and fast.

Tackling his ankles was riskier but he hadn't had time to gather himself to kick out. He was rolling in pain, clutching his knee. She shoved his other leg up so his ankles were crossed. By the time he realised what had happened, she was standing in the kitchen doorway and he was lying helpless on the living room rug, ankles and wrists solidly bound. He was swearing, cursing, crying with pain. She couldn't care. She'd done it.

She was in control.

'That'll teach you to mess with me.' She said it out loud and it was a phrase she'd rehearsed over and over, spoken in her head to him, any time these past ten years.

It felt…not good but solid. Powerful. She could cope alone. No man was ever going to mess with her again.

So stop it with the shaking, she told herself—but she couldn't.

Moving on. Call for help. How?

Her phone had been left behind. Harvey's phone? That'd be in his pocket. It'd be locked, even if she was brave enough to try and search him. Which she wasn't.

She could leave, head through the scrub to the town.

The dogs. They were prowling outside—she could hear them. There'd be barbed wire.

Somewhere in this place there'd be guns, she thought, but even if she found them… Dogs…no.

So wait.

For Harvey's mate to arrive? He knew Harvey wanted whisky. Her dad had been one of Harvey's minions. She knew how much the idiots wanted to please him—how much power he had over them. Somehow he must have managed to retain that power through his jail term.

Okay, deep breath. Don't panic. She sank back onto a kitchen chair and tried to clear a bit more of the drug-induced fog. In a couple of moments she'd go see if she could find a gun—but she needed to catch her breath first.

She needed to stop shaking, to keep this sense of control.

She needed to wait for Rab.

What sort of thought was that? Why did she think he'd come? There was no sense in it, but the thought was still there.

Rab. He'd be out in the world and he'd be hunting.

He loved her.

If worst came to worst, she could figure some way to get past the dogs. She didn't need him.

But somehow she knew that he'd come.

* * *

The chopper landed five minutes' drive from the place the cops in the nearest decent town knew as Harvey's old haunt. They'd been dubious when Brian had contacted them. 'He's been gone for years. The place was sold when he went to prison. The guy who owns it seldom comes near the place—uses it as some sort of retreat. Harvey wouldn't even have access.'

But this was a kidnapping, it was on their patch and they co-operated.

'Okay, land the chopper on the town oval,' Tom was told via the chopper radio. 'If you fly over the place, if he's there you'll put the wind up him. We'll meet you and take you from there.'

So they landed and Tom stayed—reluctantly—with the chopper. They tried to make Rab stay there too, but Brian took one look at his face and caved.

'He's a doctor, guys,' he told the local cops. 'And we're guessing she's been drugged. If she's there, who knows what we'll find.'

So two squad cars made their way to the house, with Rab in the second. They parked well back, driving off the track into the undergrowth, hiding the cars in case Harvey was yet to arrive. Was Harvey even thinking of using this place? There were so many unknowns, Rab couldn't bear to think of them. If he was wrong…where was she? He was going out of his mind.

Rab was ordered to stay with the cars, and he did, while the cops silently surrounded the house.

And then there was the sound of a car, being driven fast along the dirt track. Standing well back from the track, with the police cars in the camouflage of the bush, Rab got a glimpse of an ancient red truck.

Harvey?

He had enough sense to know he had to stay hidden. He had to trust.

And then…chaos. The screeching of brakes, tyres skidding on gravel. Frantic barking. Shouts, yelling, then loudspeakers.

'Police. Your mate's under arrest. Come out with your hands up, now.'

And Rab could bear it no longer. He was out on the track, staring at the entrance.

The red truck was slewed against the fence, the driver's door open, a cop standing over someone on the ground. The rest of the team had spread into action that was obviously part of well drilled training. Bolt cutters were slicing through the locks. Lasers stunned the dogs before they had time to attack. For all these were country cops, Rab couldn't fault them.

Another boom from the loudspeakers. 'Come out, now!'

And then, through the now open gates, he saw the front door open, just enough for someone to see what was happening. And amazingly, stunningly, it was Mia. She was still in her nurse's uniform but her feet were bare and her hair was a tangle of dark curls. Her face was pale, but when she spoke her voice was clear, with only the trace of a quaver behind the words.

'I'm safe. Harvey's here and tied up. Thank you so…so much for coming.'

It might almost be a polite thank you for calling, Rab thought incredulously, and then, even more incredulously, he realised… *She's holding a gun!* But then the police had her away from the door, taking the gun, backing her away into the shadows. There were long minutes of silence—and then, finally, a call.

'We have him. All secure, no one else here. All's well. Let the doc tend the girl.'

And seconds later—or maybe even less than seconds—Rab was in the shadows where Mia stood. Folding her into his arms.

His Mia!

He couldn't speak. All he could do was feel, and in the end it was Mia who took over.

'It's okay, Rab. I'm safe. I tied him up. I rescued me, all by myself.'

'You did.' He could hardly get the words out.

'I didn't need you. I swear I didn't.' It was as if it was a long learned mantra, a vow she couldn't break. But then there was a hiccup that sounded very much like a sob. 'But I'm... I'm so glad you came. I had Harvey but I knew his friend might come. And I found the shotgun but I didn't... I didn't think I could use it.'

'You didn't need to.'

'Because of you. I didn't have to use it because of you. It *was* you, wasn't it, who guessed where I'd be? I didn't need you but I trusted you...' Her voice broke and she buried her face in his chest.

It was so hard to make his voice work, but finally he spoke, one faltering word after another. 'Mia, you saved yourself. You're one strong woman. And, Mia, I know you don't need me, but you're my heart, my soul, and it's me who needs you. You've made me whole again, and no matter what you decide... Mia, no matter where we take this from here, I'll love you for ever.'

CHAPTER FOURTEEN

ASSAULT. KIDNAPPING. FIREARMS OFFENCES. Harvey would be put away for at least another ten years, Mia thought, and after that, she figured, there'd be no way he'd try and mess with her again.

She was free of the ogre that had haunted her all these years. She'd done it and she'd done it herself.

The lightness that followed was almost unbelievable. So many years of being under her father's control, under Harvey's control, under the boundaries of her fear... They were gone for ever—and to have Rab, desperate to find her, acting on a hunch, practically bullying the cops to take notice... It did something to her heart that she hardly recognised.

But in the hours that followed, as officialdom and documentation and blood tests and medical examination took over—as she found herself once more cast as the victim of crime—the feeling grew, becoming a sweet siren song of certainty.

This time was so different. She might have been a victim again, but she'd fought back. She'd taken control and now…now she was free to choose.

She'd been taken to hospital, like it or not. The bruises she'd received as she'd been roughly handled had been photographed, documented. Blood samples had been taken for evidence of the drug she'd been given. A gentle police-woman with a doctor in attendance—not Rab— had asked her questions, and then she'd been left to sleep.

She'd slept off exhaustion, she'd slept off the final effects of the drug, she'd slept off the last vestiges of fear.

And at midday the next day she was discharged and Tom and Brian and Rab were waiting to take her home.

Home. Wiradjuri.

They hardly spoke on the way home. Both Tom and Brian were treating her as if she were a piece of Dresden china. They didn't need to, she thought.

Oh, but she loved them. Brian was sitting beside Tom and he was beaming—what he'd achieved was huge for a country cop. Rab sat beside her in the rear. He was holding her hand as if she might be frightened of flying. Or was it that he was frightened? She sort of got it now. She felt as if she loved the whole world.

She knew she loved Rab.

She knew that fear was shared. That trust was a two-way deal. She knew that control didn't come into the equation when you truly loved.

And then the chopper was landing, and Ewan was meeting them and taking them out to the homestead.

The police had been in, searching for evidence, but once they'd finished the locals had taken over. Rhonda and Joanne and Nora were waiting, three stalwart women who took her into their arms and hugged. Boris was going nuts—as if they'd been away for months. The house was full of flowers and food, the locals welcoming her back to the valley.

Home.

And in Rab's eyes there was a tenderness, a joy—a need?

He didn't push, though. Maybe the words he'd spoken the moments after she was found were not to be repeated.

He *wouldn't* push. She knew that about him now. She'd fought so hard for control and he knew it. It was up to her.

The women left. They stood on the veranda, watching them go. Side by side. Husband and wife?

No, Mia thought. Not yet.

'Welcome home, love,' Rab said, as the last of the cars disappeared from view. There was a moment's hesitation and then his voice became careful, emotion put aside, turning to the practical. 'What do you need to do now? Have lunch? Sleep and eat later? I won't leave.'

'You can leave if you want to.'

'As can you,' he told her, and she knew he got it. He got this whole thing.

Rab. Her love.

'I am hungry,' she confessed, 'but I need to ask you a few things before we do anything else.'

'Ask away.'

And whatever the questions, whatever she asked, it was okay by him, she thought, and suddenly she grinned.

'If I asked you to do a handstand with back flip would you do it?'

There was a moment's pause. 'I might try,' he said cautiously. 'But I might well do myself some major damage.'

She smiled. 'Okay, good answer. What about climbing Mount Aranjalin?'

'You have to be kidding!' Mount Aranjalin

was a serious climbing challenge, not for the faint-hearted. Even Mia hadn't tackled it. 'No!'

That brought a chuckle and she tucked her hand into his. This felt so good. This felt awesome.

'Right, then next question. Do you think you could manage to call me Maira?'

The hold on her hand tightened. 'Do you know,' he said slowly, 'that ever since I knew your story, in my head I've called you Maira. You are Maira. You've just been hidden for a while. But now... I'm so glad you're not having to hide any more. Maira, I'm so glad you're free.'

Why did it feel as if her heart might burst?

'Well, that's three out of three, done and dusted,' she said and managed a chuckle. 'One more for a perfect score.'

'And that is?'

There was a long silence while her heart figured out how to say it. She knew what to say, but to get her tongue to say the words...?

It should be up to the guy, she thought. In stories, in movies, it was always the guy. But she'd done it once before. How hard would it be to say it again?

As Maira.

She took a deep breath, then another. Then

another, while the world seemed to hold its breath.

And while Rab waited. This was up to her, she thought. And then she thought, no. It had to be…up to them.

Gently she disengaged her hand and she stood back from him, just a little, just enough for her to read his expression. And what she saw there—this was right. It had to be right.

'I think you know what I'm about to ask,' she said softly. 'But maybe it shouldn't be my question and maybe it shouldn't be yours either. Do you think we could do it together?'

And their gazes met—and held.

He knew what she was asking. Dear heaven, he knew.

Rab stood on the sun-drenched veranda and looked into the face of the woman he loved more than anything in the world. Mia. Maira. His beautiful, life-battered, strong, courageous, gorgeous Maira. That she should ask…

That she should ask him to ask…

And it was right. No, more than right, it was the best thing in the world. The only thing. He loved this woman with all his heart. More, he needed her. Not for the practical—he knew she could cope without him, as he could cope without her. But that need was there, and it was growing by the minute.

He needed her to fill his heart. Maira.

So say it.

He took her hands again, both her hands this time, and he looked deep into her eyes. One last question, and it was the most important of all.

'My love,' he said, and his words were more a joyous proclamation. 'Maira, my love, will you marry me?'

And her voice echoed, or maybe it didn't even echo. Maybe it was said in the same breath. 'Rab, my heart, will you marry me?'

The words were spoken almost as if they'd been rehearsed, cued together, said as one.

There was a long, long silence as they stood, hands locked, looking into each other's eyes, and no vow could be made that was more powerful, more binding, than that perfect stillness.

And then the peace was broken. Right by the veranda was an ancient willow myrtle, planted deliberately so its spreading branches gave shade from the afternoon sun. On one of its lower limbs a kookaburra had obviously been watching the comings and goings with interest. Now it decided to offer its opinion. It opened its beak and a raucous chuckle rang out across the valley.

It made Rab smile, and Maira smiled right

back. And then she chuckled, and she moved against his chest and his arms enfolded her and the world was so right it was breathtaking.

But still there was one word to be said, and when he finally said it, somehow she got it, too, because the words were said in unison.

It was a good word. No, it was a great word, and it was said so loudly that for a moment even the sound of the kookaburra, and Boris's most ferocious bark as he tried to see this stupid bird off his patch, were overshadowed. Drowned out by the most important words in the universe.

'Yes.'

'Yes, I will.'

EPILOGUE

Wiradjuri, Cockatoo Valley, two years on

'"*THE MOLE WAS BEWITCHED, entranced, fascinated. By the side of the river he trotted as one trots when very small...*"'

'I know he's bright, but at eleven months maybe we shouldn't assume he knows what a mole is.'

Maira looked up from the easy chair where she'd been sitting, reading to her son. Giles was solidly asleep in his cot. His dad's birthday and the picnic down by the river that had gone with it, had been a big day in the life of a baby, and Giles had enjoyed every minute.

So had his mum and dad.

'And you do know he's asleep?' Rab asked, coming into the room to look down at his sleeping son. 'Wow. How many soft toys does one toddler need?'

'This one's the most important,' Maira said

contentedly, standing beside her husband and lifting a blue fuzzy creature with a shiny nose. 'Martin Mole. Of course he knows what a mole is. And even if he is asleep he'll still hear. I read somewhere that knowledge can ooze in while you're snoozing. I think we should start on encyclopaedias next.'

But she knew she wouldn't. Mole had marked the start of their whole wonderful relationship, and this small blue mole and the book that went with it would always make her smile. She'd fallen in love over this book. Giles might be stuck with Mole for ever.

Like she was stuck with her husband? She smiled as she thought that being stuck with this man must truly be the definition of bliss. Rab's arm came around her and together they gazed at the small, robust ball of energy that was their son.

'He looks so peaceful,' Rab said.

'He's gaining energy for tomorrow,' she warned. Giles had just learned the art of power-crawling. 'Destruction, thy name is Giles.'

He chuckled and kissed her hair. 'He's great. Let's have another.'

That was okay by her. She'd take any comers, she thought. This valley, this house, this baby, this man... Here was her joy. Here was her peace.

Here was her home.

But… 'We might already have another one,' she said now, hearing the sound of a car pulling into the driveway. It was eight o'clock on the night of Rab's thirty-seventh birthday. Robyn had promised and Robyn never broke promises.

'You mean…' Rab turned her within his arms, his eyes gleaming. He was ignoring the sound of the car in the face of much more important issues. 'Are you pregnant?'

'I would have told you if I knew,' she said, but she was metaphorically crossing her fingers. The truth was that she thought she might be, but she hadn't tested. Nor did she intend to for a day or so, because even if another baby was on the way she wanted all the attention to be on tonight's arrival.

The car was stopping at the front door and Rab was pulling away. Reluctantly. 'If this is work…'

'It can't be,' she said serenely. 'They'd have phoned.' It wasn't out of the question for Rab to be called out, though. In the two years since their 'real wedding'—a simple ceremony they'd held down by the river where they'd made vows that would hold them together for life—Rab had quietly gone about helping Cockatoo Valley Bush Nursing Hospital to become a rural medical hub. With the community buildings gifted to the community, with former leased farms sold now to locals, the valley was thriving.

One of Rab's mates from Sydney had now bought a hobby farm and was working as a family doctor-cum-anaesthetist. Two others were working as part-time doctors, and the valley was now in a position to offer internships to trainees.

Ewan could have retired content. Instead, with the injection of so much new life and energy into the valley, with the pressure eased, he'd decided to work on. 'Maybe until I'm eighty,' he'd said happily. 'Or more. I just have to wait and see.'

Ewan was on call tonight, plus one of the interns. It'd have to be a real emergency for Rab to be called out, but as the doorbell pealed and he headed out to find out what was wrong he was looking worried.

But Maira wasn't worried at all. She was smiling and smiling as she headed out to join him.

He reached the door before her. She peered past him, expecting just Robyn, but there seemed to be a crowd.

There certainly was. She flicked on the lights and saw Robyn, but she also saw Ewan. Plus his wife, Mary. Robyn's four kids were there as well, all bouncing with excitement. Robyn's husband was by her side. Joanne. Rhonda. Nora, Issy. It looked as if half the valley was either on the veranda or just below it.

'Once they knew what was happening I couldn't keep them away,' Robyn said apologetically as Maira came out onto the veranda to join her husband. Who was looking…flabbergasted.

'It seems half the valley wants to say happy birthday. And if you think you're paying for her, Maira, think again. We'd thought this might be a valley gift to both of you, but of course Hilda got in first. Do you remember Hilda, Rab? Maira's roommate in the burns unit? Hilda sends her love and says this little one is free to a good home. To your home.'

And then Robyn's Harry, now almost eighteen, a long, lanky adolescent, just accepted into medical training and with only a small white scar to show for his encounter with the blackberries, was climbing out of the back seat holding…a puppy.

Not just any puppy, Maira thought. The perfect puppy.

A small golden bundle with a white-tipped tail. She was a Labrador, but she hadn't been chosen for her breed. This little girl had been chosen for temperament, for robustness—she'd have to cope with a toddler—for compatibility with an ageing Boris...and more.

For all these years, Maira had kept in touch with Hilda, the lady who'd shared her first appalling weeks in the burns unit. When Maira had contacted her with her request, Hilda had been joyous. Yes, she remembered the gorgeous voice in the night—Dr Rab!—and if Dr Rab wanted a puppy, one of her puppies, it'd be a huge pleasure to find the perfect one. She'd listened to Maira's story with delight, and then she'd said, 'Wait.' She'd find The One.

This, then, was the result. Robyn and her family had collected the pup in Sydney yesterday and driven her home. They'd already managed a secret rendezvous with Boris—just to ensure they were compatible. As indeed they were.

And now Harry was out of the car, bringing the wriggling pup over to Rab. Handing her over. He was grinning, as was every person present.

'Happy birthday, Rab,' Maira said softly. 'Rab, meet Lulu.'

One minute he was standing on the veranda, his son sleeping in the house behind him, his wife by his side, Boris at his feet, thinking his world could never be any better than it was right at this moment. The next he was holding a soft, squirming bundle, her tongue reaching his chin for a getting-to-know-you lick, her white-tipped tail rotating like a gyrocopter in full flight.

A white-tailed dog, given to him by Hilda, and by people who cared, by people who made this place home—and by the woman at his side.

How could he ever have thought that he didn't need people? He needed every last one of those present—and more. For of course he'd noticed the way Maira had deflected his question about pregnancy. Was another new little person on the way?

But first there was this new arrival. A small dog with a white-tipped tail.

'Boris and Lulu have already met,' Maira said contentedly. 'Lulu thinks Boris is an awesome trampoline.'

'I'll bet.' But he could hardly talk—the emotions were threatening to overwhelm him. This woman... This miracle-worker...

And suddenly he was thinking of all the pain that had gone into making this moment. Maira's appalling background and her scars. The emptiness of his own childhood. The portrait of two little boys, still hanging in the living room, though joined now by the beginnings of a thousand family photographs.

'Thank you,' he said out loud, and Maira and

everyone there thought he was talking to them. And maybe he was, but he was also talking to the ghosts of those before.

'Thank you for giving me this,' he said softly, and he tugged Maira into his arms and kissed her, a great, affirming kiss that saw Lulu happily sandwich-squeezed between them. The kiss said everything that needed to be said, but finally, when they pulled apart, he found there were still words to be spoken aloud. To whoever or whatever was listening.

'Thank you for giving us our happy ever after.'

* * * * *

*If you enjoyed this story, check out
these other great reads from
Marion Lennox*

A Family to Save the Doctor's Heart
A Rescue Dog to Heal Them
Healing Her Brooding Island Hero
Falling for His Island Nurse

All available now!